MW01380525

The Compass & The Rose

NANCY ELVIRA

This is a work of fiction. Names, characters, places related to incidents are either the product of the author's imagination or are used fictitiously, and any resemblance to actual persons, living or dead, business establishments, relating to events or locales is entirely coincidental.

ISBN 978-0-692-75835-9

Cover Design by Julie D. Womack

Manufactured in the United States of America

"And you all live in my neighborhood.
How lucky for me."

The Compass
&
The Rose

He adjusted the slack in the rope, positioning himself to dive back into the water for the tail-gunner, but he was forced back and thrown onto the floor of the raft, sending the flares and an oar somersaulting over the side of the raft into the murky, green water. Layers of heavy canvas pinned him and the two pilots underneath. They were trapped, along with a few tins of water and the empty flare gun.

And only one oar.

Two seconds later, the water surrounding the raft was filled with bullets and spurting fountains of water amid ricocheting metal shrapnel. The tiny raft tipped and swayed, taking on water at a fast rate.

He struggled against the blood-soaked bags, weighing him down, fighting off the nauseating metallic taste in his mouth.

As he emerged, he let out a strangled cough. He gasped for fresh air.

His bruised and crusted face searched frantically for the pilot, his only survivor. Ears ringing, he shoved his arms up over them, attempting to escape from the pain. The agony in his joints was so intense that he didn't think he would ever be able to bring his arms back to his sides. He squeezed his eyes shut and tried to talk himself out of a breakdown.

After about 5 minutes, the sea calmed. He looked down at his right hand. More hope fleeted away; the compass needle had frozen.

Wink lay motionless on the floor of the raft, staring up at the gray sky, shrouded by gloomy, fast-moving clouds.

And he waited.

~ One ~

"TELL ME AGAIN why we are here?"

The sailor, out of breath, scurried across the parking lot after his counterpart. Realizing that he was losing the race, he paused and whined in exasperation,

"Aww ... Winston - wait up, will you!"

It made no difference; the taller of the duo showed no sign of slowing down.

"Winston!" Todd halted, completely out of breath. He removed his Dixie Cup, thinking about throwing it to the ground, but he knew that would only make things worse. He inhaled and blew out a frustrated breath.

"*Wink!* What the hell! Would you *wait up* for just a minute?"

Wink waved the papers in the air as he grumbled out loud,

"That secretary could have given me this folder four weeks ago. And I wouldn't be wasting my time coming back to this school on leave."

He stopped and flipped through the papers, studying them.

Todd caught up with him. "*Don't flip your wig*! You got your high school records. You'll still have a couple days to spend with your Granddad. Cleveland is only a few hours from here."

Wink glared back at him with an impatient frown.

They got into his 1940 *Chevrolet Special Deluxe* Convertible, and Wink hastily threw it into reverse, without first turning around to look.

A crunching sound, combined with a solid, jarring thud, sent a cold chill up his spine.

"Shit!"

Wink had backed into the Plymouth behind them, just as it was pulling forward into his space.

Which it shouldn't have been doing, either.

He pulled ahead, and then he paralleled into a space too short for his Chevy. He got out to take a better look at the Plymouth, leaving his keys in the ignition and the engine running.

There was virtually no visible damage to the Chevy; it had been often referred to by his buddies as *the tank.*

Wink assessed the situation as he got closer to the Plymouth. He reached in his shirt pocket and he pulled out a pair of half wire, half tortoiseshell eyeglasses. He positioned them on his nose, then he hunched over the driver's side to gauge the damage.

Wink ran his hand along the slight crease.

Irene didn't see him and flung open the car door, jumping out into the street, smacking him in the face with the door.

He barely flinched; he straightened up, adjusted his glasses, and rubbed his cheek.

She tripped and fell onto the pavement, landing at his feet. Her eyes widened as she shifted them upward.

Wink opened his mouth to say something, then took a good look at the flustered girl staring up at him and shut it again.

She slowly stood and moved right up to him, so close he could almost feel her breasts.

This was not at all what he had expected.

Not that he had been expecting anything. But if he had been expecting something, it would not have been what he found himself nose-to-nose with.

Her eyes were baby blue and her skin was creamy, except for the flush across her cheeks and lips.

The object of Wink's unexpected lust tilted her head slightly to the left and bit her bottom lip. He floundered around for his lost composure.

And he completely forgot about the bitch in the school office.

"I don't think it will take much to fix it; it's just a little crease." He took out a scrap of paper from his pocket and scribbled a name and address on it before handing it to her. "Stop by my uncle's shop tomorrow. He will take care of it for you. I'll talk to him this afternoon. I gave you my name too."

The cut of his biceps distracted her momentarily, as she watched him roll up his sleeves. His chest was solid; he had a strong jaw and a little indent in his chin. And he had nice hands.

"You know, you shouldn't be driving a car like this. *This is a **man's** car.*"

Winston was outrageously good-looking; his eyes were like cold steel, but she found him a bit condescending.

Irene's eyes flashed a warning at him.

She changed gears, and she became flippant. She glared at him.

"Maybe if you'd been watching where you were going, you wouldn't have hit this *man's* car," she blurted out.

He lifted his head arrogantly.

"Is that so?" he asked, rubbing his chin, with a mocking smirk.

Irene fought back the urge to stomp on his foot.

Surprised but downright charmed by the pretty young woman's straightforwardness, Wink smiled and took a step back. His first impulse was to laugh at her.

But he didn't.

In her haste to get back into her car, she stumbled again and Wink caught her by the shoulders, preventing her from taking a nasty tumble.

He pulled one hand back and steadied her with the other. She pushed his hand aside and turned up her nose.

"Well, *you* might think I am simply another one of your girls, just swooning, *all* ..." she began to sputter – "... *googly-eyed*, waiting for the chance to talk to you."

Studying her, Wink arched his eyebrows while she continued.

"Let's get something straight right now ..." She gestured freely with her hands.

"... *No sir - You better not think I'm one of them.*" she said with a nervous little laugh – a laugh that came out a lot sillier than she had intended it to be.

This girl is more than just pretty; she is sassy as hell.

The opportunity was too good for him to pass up.

Wink turned Irene toward him and met her gaze. He ran his palm slowly down her arm and clasped her hand. His eyes, like hers, softened a little. He leaned in closer and drew her into his gaze. She was like a deer in headlights.

His hand glided back up her arm, leaving a tingling path in its wake.

Her friend, Liz, almost fainted. She had been watching the whole scene from the front passenger seat of the Plymouth, but jumped out in case Irene needed backup.

Whatever spell he had cast on Irene was in full force. She tilted her eyes up to his, helplessly.

Wink's hands brushed back the loosened wisps of her hair; she melted and instinctively closed her eyes. Irene hung at his mouth, like a slave, waiting for a kiss *from him.*

Then he let go of her.

He knew exactly what he was doing.

"Well, I guess I'll see you around."

Her knees were shaking so badly that she had to lean back against Liz for stability.

Once she regained her senses, she opened her eyes – to find herself looking at Winston's back side, getting into his car, across the street. Irene darted in the opposite direction, pulling Liz along with her.

"What a horrible, *horrible* boy!"

"Well, *you* might not want to see how this ends, but *I* sure do," Liz whined, grabbing Irene tightly by the arm, dragging her back.

"*Elizabeth!*" Irene screamed, yanking her arm back, stopping them both dead in their tracks.

The whole town went quiet. Everybody, for miles in every direction, was staring at them. Irene quickly ducked behind her car and hid.

"What a dreamboat," Liz swooned. She motioned with her eyes in his direction.

"A dream is a story in your head while you are sleeping and a boat is a watercraft, and I don't see either one," Irene quipped as she stood to open the car door.

"You don't think he's handsome?" Liz whispered to Irene as they watched the car drive away.

Irene froze.

She actually did understand why Liz thought he was a dreamboat. He had the body of a Greek god and she was sure those eyes could melt an iceberg.

If they ever wanted to.

But there was no chance of that happening. She glanced at the name he had written on the piece of paper.

Winston Cunningham.

There was a rugged, rebellious look about him, yet when he had gotten close, she felt a gentle warmth radiating from him. Irene had to admit, the sailor had piqued her curiosity.

There was just one thing wrong with the picture.

The dreamboat with the wavy hair was leaving.

He had come in to her life briefly, and it was unlikely that they would meet again.

Liz laughed.

"My God, Irene, get a hold of yourself!" They got into the car and closed their respective doors.

Within a minute, the scenery changed slightly.

Winston had circled the block and found himself slowing, top back up on the Chevy, just around the corner. He stopped behind a sign. Intrigue flickered in his eyes as he leaned back in his seat, tenting his fingers.

Girls had been chasing Wink since he was fifteen, and he'd avoided monogamy ever since. Self-assured and confident, he reminded himself that he could have any girl in town.

Then why was he sitting there like a forsaken soul, hoping for one more glimpse of this one?

Clearly he was out of his mind.

Just one more glance at her; Wink's heart reacted in a short, rapid-fire fashion.

Then he drove away.

~ Two ~

"IS IT REALLY *electric*?"

Wink grinned. He reached into the car and pulled a small lever on the dashboard.

Oh, the power a convertible had over women. He could have written himself just about any ticket he wanted. He found great pleasure in the "*oohs and aahs*" as the ragtop tucked itself neatly into the rear pocket. He was just about to reveal the secret of reversing the process when he became distracted.

Wink's eyes suddenly caught a glimpse of the girl, across the street, sitting on the bench in front of the dime store.

It couldn't be ... could it?

In baggy dungarees rolled to mid-calf and a checkered shirt tied at her waist, she sat cross-legged, with her hair pinned up. Her head was lowered and she was reading a book. He felt a smile creep across his face as he watched her. Wink stared as she turned a page.

What the hell is it with this girl that's making me so crazy?

He fought back and continued dazzling his fan club, keeping one eye on the girl with the book.

He leaned into the car and ran his hand along one side of the steering wheel, stopping at the smaller control attached to it.

"It's even got a *spinner.*"

"… So, that means you have your right arm free for *other things*, right?" the blonde said with a giggle as she scooched in, behind the wheel.

One of the other girls whispered to the third one.

"… and you know what *that* means, don't you?"

Liz walked out of the store with two bags and collapsed next to Irene on the bench.

"That was close! I got the last tube of "Crimson Cherry Red" lipstick they had."

Irene laughed at her.

"I hardly think that the world would have ended if you hadn't gotten that last tube!" Liz took the stick out of the bag and twisted the base until the bright crimson greasepaint peeked out from the top.

"Irene, why don't you try some? You could use a little help."

Irene looked offended, but she rolled her eyes and laughed. They had been best friends since the second grade and this was not the first time they'd had this conversation.

She closed her book. The girls stood and began walking to the corner, where Irene's car was parked.

They stepped off the curb, but Liz quickly pulled her back so hard Irene thought they might have stepped out in front of a car. She snapped her head and looked down the street.

There he was; again.

Winston Cunningham was back.

He was facing away from them, but there was no doubt in Irene's mind that it was him. Leaning against the Chevy, he was flirting with a group of giggling girls who were listening in rapt adoration of him as he opened the driver's side door, showing off the many gauges and dials across the dashboard.

"I'll take you for a spin tonight or tomorrow, before the party," she overheard him say.

Irene's blue eyes flashed as she hurled an extremely negative thought at his back.

"Look at him, flirting, shamelessly with those little girls!"

"They're *our* age, Irene." Liz told her, rolling her eyes.

Irene bristled. "What a *Grandstander*."

She had pretty much had it with the shallowness of the male gender as of late. It had been six months since Conrad left her at the

Homecoming dance but the wound was still as fresh as if it had happened yesterday. The whole school knew he had left with Evelyn Chest.

Evelyn Chest. God had assigned her that name for more than one reason. And Irene detested both of them.

"Why are you so mad at him? He was nice to you, even when he shouldn't have been," Liz continued, pushing a piece of gum between her glossed lips. "And you were such a witch to him."

Irene shot Liz a dirty look.

"Well, it's true, isn't it?"

She had no idea how to respond to that. She turned away and rushed for her car, which wasn't far from the convertible. She held her breath.

If I can just slip away without being noticed …

But Wink saw the duo fleeing to the Plymouth. He raised his hand in a wave as he turned to face them. Irene's heart skipped a beat. Like a magnet, her eyes went directly to the dark area under his right eye.

~ Three ~

IT WAS A BEAUT of a shiner!

She pressed one hand over her chest and wiped the back of the other hand against her forehead.

Now there was no excuse. She had to go over and talk to him. *She had to!*

Wink gradually shifted his attention from his fan club to the girl walking toward him. She was nervous, but she couldn't help making eye contact as she approached him.

Wink tilted his head slightly to one side. Her expression brightened.

He smiled and looked over at her, two perfect dimples creasing his jaw, allowing his gaze to linger over the subtle curve of her hips; to her animated eyes; finally settling in on her mouth.

A gentle breeze caught a few stray strands of her hair; she pushed them to one side as she moved closer.

What really captured him; took him prisoner, was her smile. He folded his arms across his chest.

"So we meet again."

His eye was swollen, and the skin around his cheekbone was bruised. Irene felt a silly pull of attraction, but she quickly dismissed it as guilt. After all, it *was* her fault.

"Did I do that?" She gasped. "Does it hurt?"

Wink shrugged and smiled back at her.

"No, not much."

The *Wink Fan Club* slowly began to dissipate, as it became obvious that his focus had shifted. He called out to them,

"See you tomorrow at the party." They giggled in response.

Wink grinned at Irene. He propped his foot on the Chevy and he rested his hand on the edge of the windshield.

"We never did finish our conversation from the other day, did we?" He winked at her, and then winced as the bruise reminded him of its existence.

When she realized she had been playfully toying with the knot in her blouse while he was talking to her, Irene dropped it suddenly and she straightened up.

"Your uncle is a very nice man. He asked me to bring in the Plymouth tomorrow."

"So, that means you will have no car."

Irene shrugged.

"Listen, if there's any place you need to go, I will drive you."

"No, that's not necessary."

"Look, it's my fault you won't have a car. I feel responsible."

She began to walk away. "It'll only be for a few hours. I can walk." Liz wanted to choke her lights out.

Winston was losing ground fast. He had to do some quick thinking. He looked at his car, then back at Irene.

"Wouldn't you like to ride around in the *Special Deluxe*?"

That was all she needed to hear. She spun back around on her heels and faced him with a penetrating glaze.

*Just who does he think he is? I couldn't care **less** if I ever set **one foot** in his **precious car**!*

She prepared her ammunition. But when she opened her mouth, she couldn't speak.

Irene stared at him, watching the furrow deepen between his eyes as he thought about how he was going to turn this into an invitation.

He moved closer to her and, to his surprise, she didn't move away. His eyes held amusement in them.

“Listen, is it going to take an *act of Congress* to get you to go out on a date with me?” He paused and searched her face for a reaction.

He tilted her chin upward, staring into her eyes. “How about it? Tomorrow night. C’mon; a guy’s *got* to have a date for his own birthday party.”

The unexpected invitation flustered her. It was a birthday party; *his* birthday party.

Irene’s eyes danced back and forth between Wink and Liz, who was desperately trying to send telepathic signals to her; then up at the sky.

Wink’s heart pounded in his chest as he studied her. He lowered his head and slowly rotated his cap between his fingers.

She looked pensive.

And then she said yes.

~ Four ~

IN THAT UNIFORM, Winston Cunningham certainly did the United States Navy proud.

Not that he didn't look good out of uniform. He did. The light gray sweater set off his eyes beautifully.

Wink made a right turn at the stop sign. He reached over to the wood-grained panel dash and clicked on the radio, steering the red convertible with one arm across the back of the leather seat. He turned his head to Irene and chuckled.

"That bow sure looks a lot better on you than it did on the box, you know."

Irene had forgotten that Wink had tied the ribbon in her hair when he unwrapped the Philco radio, a birthday present from his aunt and uncle. With a giggle, she reached up and slid the blue bow from her auburn tresses.

The reflection from the oncoming headlights bounced around in Irene's eyes like little stars. She smiled over at him.

"That was such a nice party. Your aunt really loves you, you know."

"She's always been there for me. They both have." Wink said.

Irene sank back into the smooth leather seat and felt her whole body relax as the convertible sent them zipping down the road.

"This is so comfy. I just love everything about this car."

Wink seemed surprised at her comment.

"From the way you were acting a few days ago, I thought you hated it."

A grin blanketed Irene's face. "That was before I liked you."

Wink slowly pulled off onto a dirt road, surrounded by trees. He stopped the Chevy at a clearing near Kellar's Swimming Hole.

"Want to take a walk? The moon is nice tonight." He inhaled and followed with, "Want to see the first tree I ever climbed?"

Shit. Did I really ask that stupid question?

Irene smiled. She opened the car door and stepped out. She walked around to the front of the Chevy.

He stared at her, needing to soak up as much of her as he could before he would be gone; maybe for a long time.

In his haste, Wink realized that, although he had turned off the engine, he had left the headlights on.

"Wait here for a second," he told her and stepped back to reach into the open window. He dropped his keys. That drew a roll of his eyes and he leaned all the way in, stretching to reach the floor, where they were resting.

When Wink pulled himself back up out of the car window, he was caught completely off guard. He swallowed hard.

Irene looked at him with an expression that was hard to read.

But not for long.

She was sitting on the hood of the car, trying to hide the tube of Crimson Cherry Red lipstick she had just hastily applied.

Without a mirror.

He watched as she nervously inched her skirt up past her right thigh, her quivering fingers tugging at the hem.

Wink smiled and pulled his handkerchief from his pocket. He paused in front of her. Without a word, he gently wiped the absurd war paint from her lips.

Irene looked up at him with disappointment. She should have known better than to try to compete with what he was accustomed to looking at.

But that was not why Wink was removing the lipstick.

He just didn't think she needed it. Irene's naturally plump, red lips pushed every thought from his head straight to his groin. Winston's right temple began to throb.

After what seemed like hours, Wink closed his eyes and lowered his mouth to hers. It started out gentle and quickly became something else; something deeper.

When he broke off the kiss, they were both breathless and panting. He stood back from the car.

She slid off the hood and stood on her toes; she kissed him again. Wink hadn't yet recovered from the first one. He pulled away.

"What?" she whispered. Her eyes burned into his. He didn't answer.

She turned away, but not before he saw the hurt in her eyes.

Wink caught Irene by the shoulder and brought her into his embrace, the exchange of heat between them scorching. She molded herself tight against him.

She fumbled with the buttons on her blouse, trembling, releasing the top two. She moved on to the next one.

He pulled back; his eyes met hers. He wondered if she really knew how that could be interpreted.

This was a slippery slope if he'd ever seen one.

What could he do?

Tugging upward, his hands found the bottom of her blouse, then his mouth on her bare stomach, lips hot against her skin. She let out a whispery gasp. He gently pushed her back up onto the hood of the Chevy.

Irene was trembling, but she offered no resistance. The moonlight washed over her as he realized she must have already unfastened her brassiere; it yielded completely with his touch. Everything just fell into place.

Her eyes were shining; begging with desire.

His lips brushed her neck as his hands further explored her body; it was obvious she wanted him.

Irene's eyes appeared enormous as they traveled from Wink's eyes to his mouth and finally rested on his hand as it moved toward the belt of his trousers.

He was surprised – and angry – to feel a tinge of guilt.

This was a bad idea.

Wink forced his attention elsewhere. To *anywhere* but what was in front of him.

He sucked in a breath and he slowly took a step back.

A sob rose in Irene's throat, but she did her best to hide it. Relief and fear collided.

She was humiliated.

Wink yanked his sweater off over his head quickly and pulled it down over her. It looked huge on her tiny frame.

That's what he was hoping for.

He tucked it in tightly around her. Then he sat next to her on the hood. He pulled Irene in close, but she jerked away. He loosened the shirt collar around his neck.

"Look, I'm shipping out to the South Pacific - we might never see each other again and …"

The words died on his lips as he turned and saw what he saw.

She was crying. *Damn it!*

Irene slipped off the car and turned away from him. His sweater drooped over her body, ending at mid-thigh, drawing attention to her shaky knees. He wanted her even more than before.

Lord - What the hell else can I do to mess things up?

"You're not understanding what I am trying to say." He scrubbed his hands across his face, and looked up at the sky. She started to walk away.

He was beside her in an instant, clasping her hands in his own. He tried to meet her eyes. "Irene."

She smiled tightly and looked away. "Look at me, baby." She didn't.

"If you think for one minute that I don't … *want you* … you're wrong." Irene pressed her hand against his chest and shoved hard. He didn't budge.

Wink's heart went berserk. And, for the first time since his dog Sadie died, he cried.

Just a little bit. Because men didn't cry – everybody knew that.

Irene dropped her hand from his chest. She lost all interest in pushing him, head-first, into the pool of water.

For the next hour, they walked around the lake, holding hands. And they talked.

She learned that his dream was to be a fireman; it had been since he was 10 years old.

And that Sadie's ashes were in a cigar tin, under his bed at home. The dog had been a stray his Grandfather had taken in, but the moment she set eyes on Wink, she was his dog. Irene smiled as he pointed out the canine's name, which he had carved into the first tree he had ever climbed.

Wink was intrigued that Irene wanted to be a writer. He thought she'd make a good one.

They finally found themselves back at the car. It was getting late.

And if he didn't want to be reported as *AWOL*, he needed to be on a bus at six o'clock in the morning.

"Listen," Wink whispered in her ear. "Of course I want to touch you; be with you … in every way possible. But the time isn't right."

Irene didn't say anything. He sucked in a deep breath.

"You've never done anything like that before, have you?"

She slowly turned away from him. He pulled her close from behind, clasping his hands around her waist and spoke softly in her ear.

"You would only be doing it because I am leaving – and you think that's what I want. But that's *not* what I want. Not now."

Irene took a deep breath.

"I have no doubt that you've made your mark on many hearts," she told him.

Wink smiled and softly answered her. "But they were only pencil marks – the erasable kind."

He promised her he would write to her.

Later, standing at her front door, it felt to Wink as though he was watching a scene from a movie. She was so beautiful – even more on the inside than she was on the outside. He knew he had no choice other than to get back home to the states as soon as this whole thing was over and done with.

And make her his own.

"Mark my words - I will be back for you, Irene Walker," Wink said, between deep, lingering kisses, his heart trying to escape from his chest.

Irene looked up at Wink through a blur of tears.

She wondered how long she would carry this moment in her heart.

IRENE'S DREAMS THAT NIGHT were filled with Winston Cunningham. Her head and her fluttery heart were overflowing with tenderness and love for this young man, who was about to disappear from her life for the next year or so.

A couple of miles away, Wink growled and shoved open the door to the bathroom. He stepped inside, slammed it shut and he took a cold shower.

Even though he had already just taken one.

~ Five ~

WINK SHIFTED HIS WEIGHT as yet another person wrapped him in an embrace and mumbled words of comfort.

"Thanks for coming," he murmured, looking around the chapel, feeling guilty that he was finding himself wishing he had been able to reach Irene in time to see her before his 48-hour leave was over.

He was touched that so many people had loved his Granddad and amazed that he had helped so many.

Wink had been very close to his Grandfather. Having lost his dad when he was only eight years old, and his mother a few years later, this "mountain" of a man, a humble 70 year-old Ohio farmer had transformed himself into the role of his parent; his mentor; his idol. It wasn't until he became gravely ill that Wink was sent to Dayton to stay with a distant aunt and uncle.

Wink had never wanted anyone the way he wanted Irene.

But it wasn't just physical anymore.

He wanted to hear Irene laugh; feel her breathe. He had fantasized for months about making love to her. And to be so close, and not be able to touch her drove him insane.

And it scared the hell out of him.

~ Six ~

WINK WAS HEADING OFF on a special assignment, which meant he would not be able to send or receive mail correspondence for several months. He did tell Todd though, and asked him to give Irene a letter he had written to her, explaining it all.

The letter was easy to write. More difficult was the problem of making sure it would reach Irene.

He drummed his fingers on the table.

"You're sure you'll get to Dayton before you go to Norfolk?"

Todd nodded. "My parents are expecting me to spend my liberty with them." Todd had been recently promoted to the rank of Seaman First Class and he was being sent stateside on another assignment.

Wink sealed the envelope and relinquished it to him. He wondered how Irene would react when she read it.

In the letter, Wink told Irene that he loved her, and that he couldn't imagine spending the rest of his life with anyone else.

Todd put on his cap and they shook hands. Wink shielded his eyes with his hand as tiny particles of debris skittered across the surface of the aircraft carrier.

The whirring of propeller blades shook the air as Todd slung his sea bag over his shoulder, pivoted and walked toward the waiting helicopter.

WINK DARED TAKE only one sentimental item along with him on the assignment, as that was forbidden.

Forbidden, yes; but they all did it.

He folded the last letter he had received from Irene and stuffed it inside his sea bag. Then he took it back out and tucked it in the pocket of his shirt for safekeeping.

In the letter, she had promised to wait for him.

Forever.

~ Seven ~

CHIEF PETTY OFFICER Winston Cunningham and his team had flown out on a search-and-rescue mission to find a crew that had reportedly crashed.

A few hundred miles south of Hawaii, their plane ran into deep trouble. One of the engines suddenly failed, followed closely by the engine on the opposite side.

It played out like one unbroken stream of chain reactions; the whole thing was like a whirlwind.

The plane plummeted.

They spiraled out of control, hit the water, and then went into a heart-stopping cartwheel.

And then the plane shattered.

~ Eight ~

WINK LANDED HARD, on his left shoulder, then again on his face. When he opened his eyes, completely disoriented, he was surrounded by a tangle of metal spaghetti. There were cables and wires everywhere he looked.

It was a scene Wink would never quite be able to obliterate from his mind.

An eerie creak echoed throughout the sinking fuselage, followed by an ominous groan.

He was finally able to squeeze himself out of the plane; the skin scraping off his arms and shoulders as he stuffed himself and a radio through a hole in the fuselage. He surfaced to find fire, smoke and debris on the water.

Wink inflated his life jacket. He spotted his pilot and co-pilot clinging to a fuel tank about 30 feet away.

He grabbed a pile of rubber, struggling against the water's force. While it first offered resistance, the CO2 canister finally triggered, and the rubber transformed into a life raft. He struggled over the side and rolled onto the floor.

Wink grabbed the oars and quickly navigated his way over to the pilots.

He wedged his leg between the severed wing and the fuel tank, to keep the shredded metal from piercing either one.

Without warning, a large piece of twisted fuselage hit the amputated wing and forced the two together, crushing Wink's ankle.

The pain was agonizing; he wasn't sure he could continue, but he kept going.

He was able to pull the pilot over onto the floating wing. He breathed a sigh of relief when he saw him open his eyes; quickly rolling onto his side, vomiting.

But it was an entirely different story with the co-pilot.

Wink pressed a soaked towel against his chest.

His eyes were open, the light in them fading. He took a shuddering breath. And then nothing.

Wink desperately tried resuscitating him but it was no use; his heart just couldn't take any more. He quickly shuffled both of the young pilots from the broken wing into the raft.

He adjusted the slack in the rope, positioning himself to dive back into the water for the tail-gunner, but he was forced back and thrown onto the floor of the raft, sending his flares and an oar somersaulting over the side of the raft into the murky, green water. Layers of heavy canvas pinned him and the two pilots underneath.

They were trapped, along with a few tins of water and the empty flare gun.

And only one oar.

Seconds later, the water surrounding the raft was filled with bullets and spurting fountains of water amid ricocheting metal shrapnel. The tiny raft tipped and swayed, taking on water at a fast rate.

He struggled against the bags drenched in saltwater and blood, weighing him down, fighting off the nauseating metallic taste in his mouth.

As he emerged, he let out a strangled cough. He gasped for fresh air.

His bruised and crusted face searched frantically for the pilot, his only survivor. Ears ringing, he shoved his arms up over them, attempting to escape from the pain. The agony in his joints was so intense that he didn't think he would ever be able to bring his arms back to his sides. He squeezed his eyes shut and tried to talk himself out of a breakdown.

After about 5 minutes, the sea calmed. He looked down at his right hand. More hope fleeted away; the compass needle had frozen.

Wink lay motionless on the floor of the raft, staring up at the gray sky, shrouded by gloomy, fast-moving clouds.

And he waited.

He was convinced that the low, thick cloud ceiling was playing a big part in keeping him hidden; alive. He checked the pilot again for a pulse. He was still breathing, but fading. Wink thought he spotted a B-25, but it didn't see them.

His flare gun was worthless; his compass had frozen. What else could go wrong?

Wink had just about run out of hope. He felt himself collapse against the side of the raft, leaning over the edge, his fingers digging into the side.

He listened to nondescript sea life rubbing along the raft bottom.

How long would it be before the sharks found them?

Wink's delirious mind played tricks on him for the next few moments; he heard the sea claiming him … calling his name.

He dreamed about drowning – then being snatched back, off the one-way path leading to the burial ground of the Pacific floor.

The sky was dark. Lightning bolts hit the atmosphere as thunder in the distance continued in deafening waves.

Winston was reeling, his head in a heavy cloud, as if he had been drugged. Water crested over the sides of the raft, sloshing over everything in its way, while eerie visions floated past him.

Vague words, smudged across the side of the broken plane, appeared and disappeared, only to reappear again amid the waves of sea mist and thickening fog.

Water lapped rhythmically against the raft while the air, heavy like pea soup, dropped over the sides with each dip.

With no physical means of steering, Wink knew the craft would sail, helplessly, in the direction of the wind.

To the south, gunfire flashed in the night sky. It drew closer. Wink closed his eyes and slipped into unconsciousness.

~ Nine ~

THE RADIO CRACKLED to life with a voice.

"*Little Black Tail* – Do you copy?"

Silence followed. Wink was too weak to sit up and look for the source of the voice.

The radio jumped back to life again.

"*BLACK TAIL! Are you there?*"

His hand was dangling over the side of the raft. The spray from the sea air stung the lacerations on his back, face and his arms. His lips were burned and cracked. More than 24 hours had passed.

The distant roar of an engine, growing more distinct by the second, shook the air.

Wink saw a light from an aircraft in the distance; a monoplane flying low in and out of the fog.

Approaching from the northeast, the pilot released two flares. Winston dragged himself to the middle of the raft and raised his arms above his head, waving with the hope that it was friendly.

Within minutes, Wink saw that the plane had floating pontoons, and was blinking a code signal. He hoped he wasn't hallucinating as it performed a short glide and settled down on the water not far from the raft.

Relieved, he recognized the star on its side as the US Navy flying boat got closer.

It taxied over and the pilot cut the engine. As Wink grabbed hold of one of the plane's pontoons, a flier climbed out to assist him.

With a renewed sense of energy under his belt, Wink secured his pilot's broken body to a board, then observed as he was secured aboard the plane.

Then he fought back tears as he covered the co-pilot's lifeless body with the stained cloth and watched as he was lifted and safeguarded into the rear of the aircraft.

His heart pounding wildly in his chest, briny air filling his lungs, Wink waved his arms around and shouted,

"Gunner! *I have to find my gunner!"*

The pilot shook his head and replied with a sense of urgency. *"No time! We've got to get out now*!"

When he saw the look on Wink's face, he hollered, "We'll find him, Chief. Maybe not now - but we will find him!"

Wink climbed into the PBY through the hatch, where he collapsed onto a cot. The airman looked at Wink's injured ankle.

"We've got to get that foot taken care of, Chief, *ASAP*."

Wink looked down at his twisted, discolored foot. He had forgotten about his injury.

Once aboard the aircraft carrier, Wink hobbled forward before hastily being thrown onto a gurney. The salt air biting at his exposed, raw flesh, he was whisked off to sick bay. He was in excruciating pain, but grateful to be alive.

Wink was unstrapped from the gurney and transferred to a cot.

IN HIS INTERVIEW, he was asked about his signal to the plane. There was an unusual interest in the SOS that Wink had transmitted to alert the plane.

And they wanted to know what kind of flare gun he had used to signal them – it was unlike anything any of them had ever seen before.

Wink explained to them that he had no flares; that they had gone overboard. And that he could not remember anything after he lost consciousness until the radio communication and the plane appeared.

The crew was stumped. The officer attending to him mouthed, in a surprised whisper,

"What? How is that possible?"

Wink's stomach churned. He forced down another cracker.

The search for any remaining survivors was temporarily suspended.

~ Ten ~

THAT NIGHT, WINK woke in a cold sweat, the odor of death still fresh in his head. He was overcome by an overwhelming and hopeless sense of dread and anxiety.

And then he remembered.

The plane wreck; the badly maimed pilot he had pulled from the wreckage; the eyes of the one he could not save, staring back at him. And the one he never even reached. His mind played unkind tricks on him as it replayed the visions on a repeating loop.

Being part of many search and rescue operations, Wink should have become desensitized to it; he'd certainly seen the sea give up more than its fair share of the dead. But it never got easier.

He yelled out as he leaped up from the cot, violently retching stomach bile into the utility bucket at his bedside. The pain from his splintered ankle, which had been freshly plastered, was too much to bear.

Solid hands guided him back toward the cot. In a kind voice, the corpsman gave him the encouragement he thought Wink needed.

"Chief – the cast will never last if you don't give it a chance to set."

Wink's face twisted with pain as he instinctively groped for the ball chain around his neck, but it wasn't there.

Dog tags! Wink lost it and curled his hands into fists. *"My Dog Tags are gone!"*

He panicked.

The attending medic calmly reassured him, guiding him back onto the cot. "Don't worry; they can be replaced." Then he reached into an envelope and handed Wink something.

"Look; here's your compass – it was in your hand when you were rescued. Just relax. Everything's fine."

Wink reeled as the medic placed the compass in his hand and clasped his fingers tightly around it.

It wasn't until later that evening, when Wink opened his fist, he realized that the weathered and corroded compass he was holding was not *his*.

~ Eleven ~

IT RAINED ON HIS first morning back in Dayton, Ohio.

Wink stood up as the train chugged in on screaming brakes.

As he descended the steps of the passenger car, Wink looked around and took in as much of his surroundings as his brain would absorb.

He was home.

Wink appeared on the platform. As the smoke cleared, his smile grew wider.

Naturally, his aunt cried and held on to him, while Uncle Hank blinked back a stray tear. Only when he got close enough to see Wink's eyes did his uncle give in to the emotion of the moment, slinging an arm around his shoulders.

Just a few minutes had passed by before he searched around and asked the question.

"Is Irene here?"

His aunt's eyes flashed over at his uncle, whose face held an uncomfortable, helpless expression.

Aunt Dolly did her best to change the subject, focusing instead on Wink's ankle. She kissed his cheek and said,

"Honey, let's just get you home and off that foot for little while."

Wink sensed she was hiding something. He had gone too long without seeing Irene already. He had no intention of granting an extension. He grabbed his aunt's hand as they got into the car.

"Aunt Dolly – Stop avoiding my question. Have you seen Irene?"

Dolly patted Wink's hand and said, "Honey, she was just a very nice girl you met right before you went away. Those short relationships rarely last."

Wink knew something was wrong. Even though Irene had ignored the letter Todd had given to her months ago, he at least thought his aunt would have contacted her to tell her he was on his way home.

And that she might want to greet him at the train station, or something.

Anything.

Silence shrouded the majority of the car ride home. Wink's mind was turning over a million miles a minute with scenarios of what could have happened.

As Hank pulled into the driveway, Dolly jumped out to unlock the front door. Wink leaned over the front seat and quizzed his uncle.

"Would somebody *please* tell me where Irene is?"

Hank turned around and faced Wink. He took in a deep breath.

"Irene's daddy picked the whole family up and moved to Cleveland."

Wink nearly jumped out of his skin.

"When?" Hank hesitated. Wink grabbed his arm. "I said *when?"*

"A few months ago."

Wink flung the car door open. He hobbled to the front door. The second he stepped into the house, he turned to Dolly and said,

"I want to go into town to send a telegram … Will you help me?"

~ Twelve ~

WINK STOPPED DEAD in his tracks in the street when he recognized the curves of Irene's silhouette on the porch with a man. Then he heard her voice.

The blast of a horn from a pickup truck, barely missing the stunned stranger in the street, startled Irene. She turned her head, and she froze.

Irene clamped her lips tight, staring in disbelief from the porch at the man in uniform, across the yard. He was thin, but just as handsome as the day he first caught her eye after their little accident. As Irene realized who he was, she slowly rose to her feet. She stood very still, waiting for Wink to speak.

He didn't.

"You're here!" Irene's tears flowed freely as she jumped down the porch steps into the street, flinging herself into his arms.

Wink winced with pain from his ankle, but he welcomed Irene in his embrace. He didn't push her away. In fact, he held onto her tightly. They clung to each other for a few minutes – her face pressed against his jacket, she swallowed burning sobs as she sniffed his unforgettable fragrance.

She leaned back, still in his embrace.

"You look so … tired," Irene told him, staring at the circles under his eyes.

But Wink quickly stiffened, remembering that Irene had moved on to another man without answering the letter he had sent to her.

The letter he had sent with Todd.

He sighed and turned away, but quickly spun back, facing her again.

"I thought you were going to wait for me. What happened? *Some promise, I tell you!"*

Irene bit her lower lip. "I believe you just implied I'm a liar!" She began to tear up again. *"Me??* What about *your* promise, Winston?! I sent you a letter every day for three months with no answer! You just stopped writing me back … without as much as an *"I'll see you around!"*

Irene closed her eyes tight, in a failed attempt to prevent more tears from escaping. She felt Wink's fingers on her cheek.

She opened her eyes and saw a softness in his, staring back at her, intently. She held her breath, trying not to cry. She looked down at Wink's hand covering her own.

She sniffled and continued, "When you stopped answering my letters, I didn't believe I could ever go on breathing … or that my heart could go on beating."

Wink raised an eyebrow and turned his head to the porch.

Todd immediately looked away from him.

"And Todd helped me put my life back together again. He made me feel needed; and *wanted.* Honestly Winston; what did you *think* I would do? … *never* get married because you broke my heart?"

Wink's limp morphed into a swagger as he headed for the porch steps and hesitated for only a moment.

... The letter I sent to Irene with ***Todd*** *...*

His face burned with anger and he forgot all about his ankle.

Wink inhaled a sharp breath and jumped right into the quagmire, taking two steps at a time, Irene on his heels, until he was on the porch, face-to-face with Todd. He breathed louder and harder.

"Tell me again why you are here?"

~ Thirteen ~

TODD STEPPED AWAY in alarm and made a dash toward the porch steps.

At that exact moment, Wink propelled himself at the traitor, his shoulder knocking over the table, sending the lemonade pitcher and glasses crashing to the plank floor.

Bedlam ensued as the duo scrambled to position themselves for the fray that was about to happen.

The force of Wink's backward swing at Todd's face, threw him off-balance, causing him to turn his foot. His ankle exploded in pain as he attempted to regain his balance; he fell on the broken glass and tumbled down the steps to the grass.

Irene screamed Wink's name at the top of her lungs.

She rushed down the stairs, followed closely by Todd. Irene kneeled at his side.

Wink didn't move - his eyes were closed; he couldn't bring himself to open them at the moment.

Nice going. You made it through one of the most intense battles of the whole war, and you died falling down six lousy porch steps. What an embarrassing way to go.

Irene scowled up at Todd, confused and furious.

Todd panicked as he peered down at Wink's lifeless body. What the hell had he done? Wink had always been like a brother to him – ever since they were in grade school. Beads of sweat quickly formed on his brow. Whimpering, he crouched down and reached out to touch his best friend's face.

But Todd's right hand was met with the bone crushing grip of Wink's left hand. Wink's eyes popped open as he grasped Todd's forearm, struggling to stand. The look on his face was unmistakable.

He was enraged.

Wink jerked away from Todd once he was steady on his feet. Todd swallowed hard and asked in a trembling voice,

"Does it hurt?"

Wink's eyes hardened. "No, not much."

And with that, Wink spun back around on his splintered ankle, drew back his blood-covered fist and let Todd have it, square in the face, sending him on a nonstop flight across the yard into the rose bushes.

Blood spewed from Todd's nose as Wink yanked him back to his feet and threw him onto the grass. The sting of anger on his face dissolved into satisfaction.

With a wicked grin, Wink wiped the blood from his mouth with the back of his hand, spit a mouthful onto the ground and turned back to face Todd, who was rolling around in the grass, and he asked the question,

"Does it hurt?"

Todd sat up, holding his nose, without looking at him. And in a barely audible voice, he answered, "No, not much."

Wink looked over at the collection of stunned neighbors that had assembled on the street.

"Sorry for the disturbance, folks." Then he fell to the ground again, his compromised plaster cast forcing his ankle inward.

Irene dropped to his side, sobbing. She reached to release his foot from the bind.

"*Ow!* My ankle!"

"Stop thrashing around. You're just making it worse," Irene said.

"It's throbbing like hell."

Wink watched her eyes as she rolled his pant leg up past the damaged cast. His hand tightened on hers.

Yes; he was still in love with her – maybe even more now than before.

"You know, you should come with a warning label." He winked at her.

"I think you're the one who needs the label," Irene whispered, wedging herself behind Wink for support as he attempted to stand again. She turned her head up to him. He suddenly realized that he hadn't even kissed her yet. He couldn't help himself.

Her mouth was as sweet as he remembered.

The silhouette of Irene's mother suddenly appeared on the other side of the screen door.

"Irene – you aren't going to believe who your father just got a cable from." She followed with a gasp. "***Good Lord***, what in the world is going on out there?"

~ Fourteen ~

THEY WERE LYING on a blanket, outside of his grandfather's house. The fall sun had just set.

Irene was watching fireflies flutter through the grass. She rolled over onto her stomach, studying his closed eyes, his mouth; the recent injuries to his face. She tickled him under his nose. He opened his eyes and quickly flipped her over onto her back. One side of her face gilded by the slipping sun, Wink leaned over her.

She tugged down self-consciously at the hem of her dress, which had ridden up, exposing her panties.

Now he was the one who was staring.

The moment gripped them, and Irene closed and opened her eyes to make sure it was real. Wink leaned back, still holding onto her. They smiled at each other. She didn't want to let go of his arms for fear he might disappear.

He couldn't imagine a life without her, before or after the South Pacific. She was a force of nature. Wink kissed Irene, trying to use restraint, using his tongue to show her what he would like to be doing to the rest of her body.

There were a hundred reasons why they shouldn't do what they were thinking about doing.

But there were a million why they should.

Wink's re-cast ankle was still painful, but he scooped Irene up in his arms and carried her into the house. He hesitated for a moment to lock the door.

Her mind swirled, and her body tingled with sensations she had never felt before. Irene felt a shiver run down her spine as Wink dropped her onto the bed.

He wondered if her heart was beating as hard as his. He pressed her hand to his chest, and she took his hand and did the same. Wink caught his breath. He leaned in again and kissed her. His lips were gentle, his arms enfolding her in a way that made her want him to never, ever let go.

Then Wink kissed Irene again, this time deeper, as if he had just discovered that he was alive. His mouth opened, parting her lips with an unquenchable desire matched only by hers.

~ Fifteen ~

IRENE WOKE WITH her head nestled against Wink's shoulder, his arm tightly around her. She felt cozy and warm, her fingers idly tracing the line of his rib.

But as she brushed her unruly hair away from her face, she suddenly remembered last night.

Irene sat straight up. Her frantic eyes flew open. Heat rushed across her scalp.

She was in Winston's grandfather's house – in the bedroom; in the bed.

And she was naked.

Her gasp awakened Wink from his deep slumber. It was the first time in fourteen months that he had slept past sunrise. He reached for her and pulled her back on top of him. He whispered against her hair.

"I love you, Irene Walker."

She tried to look away. He could see the dread settle over her.

Wink gently flipped her onto her back and he winked, caressing her cheek with his fingers. She felt soft and vulnerable in his arms.

"And I'm pretty sure you love me, too."

Then she quickly sat up again. "Do you think everybody knows?" Irene released a faint sob and wrapped her arms around his neck.

Wink comically stroked his chin, preparing to pontificate. He winked and smiled at her.

"You know what this means, don't you?"

She didn't answer. He grinned and continued.

"To protect my reputation, you're just going to have to marry me."

She couldn't look at him – she just continued weeping softly.

"Irene?" He wasn't sure why she was crying.

Wink suddenly realized what a knucklehead he was. That was not the way any self-respecting woman wanted to hear that her guy loves her.

He jumped up out of bed and ran to the window. He flung open the curtains and attempted to break the lock. He pounded on the sash.

Irene quickly sucked her tears back in, transforming them into emergency energy. She flew after him, noting that he was completely naked.

"Wink! What are you trying to do?"

"I want to tell the world that I love you!"

The warmth that had prickled her scalp dropped to her stomach. She gave him a silly cockeyed grin. Her eyes gave him a quick *once-over.* Her smile grew wider.

"Go ahead. I'm sure the spinsters next door would enjoy the view."

Wink looked down at himself; then back at her. "You don't have anything on either."

She winked at him. "Yes, but I am not standing in front of the window." Wink jumped and quickly dropped the curtain back over the window.

He grabbed Irene and locked her in his embrace. They lost their balance, falling into a pile on the floor, laughing uncontrollably.

She pulled back and she smiled. "We deserve each other, don't we?"

He winked at her. And he said nothing else.

No more words; he was shitty with those anyway.

~ Sixteen ~

THE IVORY TEA-LENGTH gown fit Irene like a glove.

In the weeks leading up to the wedding, Wink and Irene had been so swept up by friends and family, they were happy to see the day finally arrive.

They had settled on a small Saturday afternoon ceremony, with family and about a dozen friends in attendance.

Judge Warner, who had known Wink's grandfather for years, and his wife hosted the wedding at their home on the near west side. The officiant of the ceremony, the judge had insisted upon having a reception at his house.

Irene's mother dabbed her eyes with a hanky, then tucked it into the belt of her dress as she watched the touching interaction between Wink and her little girl throughout the ceremony.

Hank kept his arm around Dolly's shoulders, secretly studying her face. He agreed with the guests that Irene was the most beautiful woman in the room.

That was, except for Dolly. But the attention was supposed to be on the bride, so he wisely kept his personal thoughts to himself.

Dolly and Hank had never been blessed with children, so when Wink came to live with them, he became their family. And now, there was one more. It was a joyous occasion. There was so much to look forward to.

Irene's mother held onto her husband who, much to his surprise, was more emotional than anybody thought he would be. He found it very difficult to speak without choking up at the significance of the day. He was very happy, but he felt a little like he was losing his daughter. He watched his wife from across the room as she mingled with the wedding guests.

She and Dolly had become close friends over the recent weeks and were happy that they were not only best friends now, but family.

IRENE AND WINK'S wedding night didn't disappoint either one of them. It wasn't until the wee hours of the morning that they finally fell asleep in each other's arms.

About two hours later, Irene was awakened by Wink, who was tossing and turning in bed.

She gently touched his shoulder to try to wake him, but he continued to toss and turn, mumbling in his sleep.

"Wink," she whispered against his ear. A calmness seemed to come over him. Concerned, she caressed his forehead, wiping away the beads of sweat that had formed.

He must have sensed she was watching him. He opened his eyes and after a moment, he turned to her.

"Did I wake you up?"

Irene smiled and she lied. "No, I was already awake."

Wink sat up and ran his fingers through his hair while Irene rubbed his back. She inhaled and asked him,

"Do you want to talk about it? It might help."

He faced her, and then turned away. "I have this nightmare; not all the time, but it's always the same dream."

Irene gently guided him to lie back down on the bed. She motioned for him to roll over and she began to massage his back.

"Tell me about your dream."

"I started having it after the plane crash."

Irene felt him relax a little, and then he turned over on his back to face her.

"It's just like … I am back there, all over again; the crash, the struggle to stay alive. The fog that chokes me … and it always ends just as I start to read the words on the side of that damn plane."

"What words do you see?"

Wink squeezed his eyes shut. "That's just it. I never see the whole thing – just parts of it." He wiped his hand across his mouth and continued.

"I can make out an SS, but I can never figure out the rest of it." He sat up again and folded his arms across his chest.

"I don't know why I keep having that same dream. I just don't understand it." He shrugged in a self-deprecating way and added,

"It's not important."

Irene tried to disguise her concern. They lay back down on the bed and she smiled over at Wink.

"It *is* important. We'll figure it out together." Wink was her hero and nothing could ever change that.

She watched him until she was certain he had drifted back off to sleep.

~ Seventeen ~

NESTLED BETWEEN DOWNTOWN and the far western border of Cleveland, Edgewater Park was viewed as an idyllic destination by the numerous visitors that flooded its shores every summer. But to those who lived in the Edgewater community, it was home; a symbol of beauty and rich with history.

Wink lay in bed on a chilly Saturday morning, the covers pulled up to his chin. He smiled over at Irene as he quietly slipped out of bed, careful not to wake her.

It was the middle of January and the weather had turned bitterly cold. The sky had given up all trace of blue, waiting for the freezing rain to turn to snow.

He found it hard to believe it had been nine years since they had been married. It seemed like only a few years had gone by.

His grandfather's house had sold the day after Wink joined the City Fire Department, one year following his discharge from the Navy. He and Irene had been renting their brownstone apartment in the Edgewater area for nearly eight years.

Glistening pine trees grew close to the roadside, hugging the cliff face, as Wink made his daily hike along the Lake Erie shoreline. He never tired of the view, discovering something new on each walk.

He knew the old logic behind the plan; why the first settlers had built Cleveland along the lake and the river. It had little to do with the pretty view and everything to do with practicality.

The cold air had brought along a crisp and fresh scent of snow. He slapped both hands against his frozen cheeks, hoping to circulate the blood in his face. He blew on the tips of his fingers, and then he reached in his pockets for his gloves to rescue his icy hands.

Wink's routine trek typically included a visit to the 9th Street Pier to shoot the breeze with the collection of fishermen and, on weekends, to visit with a tugboat captain or have an occasional cup of coffee at the Coast Guard Station.

On that particular day, Wink was running behind and he decided to take a different route; a shortcut, closer to the cliffs than his usual path.

Thankful that his boots had treads deep enough to grip the snow-covered incline to the street above, Wink was pleased that he had trimmed at least fifteen minutes off his estimated time of arrival. He shook the snow from his pant legs and straightened up, facing the street in front of him.

Wink stared directly ahead and froze. His eyes were drawn in by a sign posted in the front yard of a house facing the lake.

– A *For Sale* sign he hadn't seen before.

~ Eighteen ~

HE FORGOT ALL ABOUT being late and wandered across the street. Wink studied the property.

Sandwiched in between a massive Tudor and a classic Arts and Crafts bungalow, it was obvious that the old house needed help.

Oriented to take in the best views of its long neglected garden and the lake, the structure was built of cool, polished stone and russet bricks, with several graceful, steep-pitched, swooping roofs.

It was wildly overgrown; what Wink liked to call a *diamond in the rough,* but a real treasure.

The morning sunlight danced on the beveled glass edges of the transom windows, drawing attention to their sapphire blue stained glass accents. A long gutter hung over the front step by a piece of entwined wire.

Whatever color the paint covering the railing of the porch had been was barely recognizable and, in places, was gone completely.

Winter-dead roses entwined a trellis, looking like they died trying to escape. There was one tangle of roses inching its way up the side of the house; a few survivors; but mostly dried up. He didn't pay much attention to them. But he knew Irene would have appreciated them.

In the midst of the January Cleveland winter, it all looked a little sinister to Wink, but he knew come spring, the trellis would be covered in green sprouts that would soon explode into a fragrant vertical utopic garden.

At least that's what Irene would have said.

He looked up at shingles that were beginning to curl and climbed the cracked concrete steps to the front door. He paused to open the splintered wood screen and tapped the door knocker.

When no one answered, he knocked again, then shaded his eyes and peered through the leaded glass door. Wink was about to ring the bell when he saw someone through the glass. He put his hand down. The door opened slowly and an older man appeared, reluctantly.

"Yes?" He shifted his head slightly as if he could hear better with one ear than the other. His weathered face was lined like a road map.

Wink smiled and extended his hand out to the man. "Good morning, sir. My name is Winston Cunningham."

The man did not reciprocate. Without expression, he spoke in a monotone dialect. "You would be interested in the house, would you?" No smile; no sign of warmth.

Wink retracted his hand. It was almost as if the old guy didn't like him.

What kind of person doesn't like somebody he's never met? This is going to require some work – this man is clearly screening potential buyers to fit a specific criteria.

And he had no idea what that was.

Wink was eventually invited into the house.

The door opened into a hallway, with a breathtaking Mahogany staircase, slightly to the right. His eyes lifted to the vaulted ceiling. As he wandered into the foyer, he found himself drawn to its personality, the craftsmanship put into the house; its creation and its history.

Then he noticed the beautiful hardwood floors, gleaming in the pale sunlight and the floor to ceiling windows along the front of the house. But when he was led into the living room, his jaw dropped.

The built-ins were beautiful, from the leaded-glass panels set into the cabinets to the hand-hammered escutcheons and finger loop pulls.

Framing a breathtaking view of the city was a magnificent window with stained-glass bays in its upper sashes that was impossible to ignore. Wink hadn't noticed the detail from the outside. He walked to the window and stood still.

The lake stretched from one end of the room to the other, in a kaleidoscope of grays and blues. Before he could stop himself, he blurted out,

"Why are you selling this place?"

The man walked over to the window, and turned his back to Wink. He wondered if that gesture and his silence were meant to indicate that he had crossed some sort of line with his question.

But, what line had he crossed?

Had he stumbled upon a sore spot that the old man had buried over the years? Or did he just think Wink was inappropriately nosy?

He found himself getting lost in the view from the window. It was like being at the helm of a ship out on the sea. Standing there, he could almost feel the ship's wheel in his hands, the brisk air stinging his face.

At the base of the window was a seat with a cushion upholstered in a sapphire blue damask fabric – too exquisite to have been made stateside. Wink leaned over and touched it, ever so slightly.

For reasons Wink didn't understand, the man suddenly turned back to the window, then quickly pulled the drapes closed. He gestured to Wink to follow him as he exited the living room. Wink stopped and ran his hand over the edge of the fireplace mantel, a flawless chunk of cherry that had been wedged into the stones. He continued, walking backwards, following the old man into the hallway.

The man led him up the staircase. Wink stopped half way up to look at a portrait on the wall; a painting of a beautiful young woman.

He was mesmerized. The face of an angel, yet something so sensuous about her that he found himself flushed. Around her neck was an exquisite pendant, embellished with jewels.

The man kept going, but he glanced back when he saw that Wink was fixated on the framed portrait. A weary smile spread across his wrinkled face as he observed Wink. He nodded.

"She's beautiful. Who is she?" Wink inquired.

The man stepped back down to just above him. "That's Kathleen." He smiled and added, "Kathleen Rose."

"Did she live here?"

"Yes." He looked straight ahead, emotionless. "This was Katie's home." His voice trailed off and he continued up the staircase, without another word.

Each new detail Wink learned about the house made it stand apart even more from the last. The four bedrooms were unique; each had a floor made from a different hardwood.

Coming back down the stairs to the landing, staring backward at the painting on the wall, Wink nearly tripped on the corner of a circular Persian carpet; a rug so threadbare there was almost no pile left.

He kneeled down to flatten the corner, but instead of straightening out the fold in the carpet, he found himself rolling the edge back even further.

Wink was awe-struck.

At the base of the worn, varnished wood floor, hidden underneath the rug, was an inlaid design. A compass.

A *Compass Rose*.

He recognized it immediately; it was one of the first things he learned about while he was in the Navy. Obviously the work of a master craftsman and, although it was dirty, it had been preserved beautifully.

The Compass Rose was designed in a fashion that resembled a flower; the rose. It helped to orient a map in the correct direction and gave the relative directions for points on the chart.

Before the rose was used on maps, lines were drawn from points. These lines were hard to follow since there were usually several of these lines intersecting each other on one map. The rose design was drawn in a way that made it easier to follow the directional lines.

Wink traced the outline with his fingers.

He had an eerie feeling that he was being watched. He looked around, but the man was nowhere to be found.

Wink remembered the portrait on the staircase wall. He glanced up, as he climbed a few steps to see if his hunch was correct.

Sure enough; it was. The pendant around the beautiful woman's neck was a jewel-encrusted Compass Rose.

The old man suddenly reappeared, at the base of the staircase. He freely gestured with his hand, without speaking, leading Wink back down the corridor and up a separate set of steps behind the hallway into a room with a desk and a large bay window.

The walls were lined with bookcases, filled with old leather-bound volumes, screaming to be opened and read cover-to-cover.

While beautiful, Wink couldn't help thinking that every square foot of the place was in varying degrees of dilapidation.

The man seated himself at the massive mahogany desk, steepling his fingers; contemplating. He remained silent for a few moments. He looked intensely at Wink.

He didn't invite him to sit down, but Wink sat down anyway, in one of the rich, leather-upholstered chairs across from the desk. The man stared at Wink. Then his gray eyes twinkled at his own words.

"You don't intimidate easily, do you?"

"Sir?" Wink was surprised at the comment.

"Cleveland winters are endless and summers are a blur."

Wink didn't hesitate. "Yes sir – I was born and raised in Ohio."

The man abruptly jumped up from behind the desk and walked to the door, out into the hallway. Wink followed. When they reached the top of the stairs, the old man took one step down, then turned back to face Wink.

"The house is yours, if you still want it."

Wink's mouth dropped open. He hadn't expected things to unfold quite in this way. He stammered a little, and then he inhaled deeply.

"I would have to bring my wife over to see it first."

"Naturally."

They left through the kitchen door and walked through what had once been an elegant garden. Wildly overgrown now with choking weeds, it looked to him like it had just given up the ghost.

On the other side of the driveway, there was a dilapidated building with a highly-pitched roof. At the side of the structure was a door, secured with a padlock.

The man stopped and looked up at a window.

"Nothing up in that attic – been empty for years. No need to even go up there now."

Wink wondered if the man was hiding something; like maybe a dead body. He thought about insisting that he have a chance to go up and investigate. But he reconsidered.

Even if the old carriage house was falling down, the house was still worth it. He didn't want to run the risk of changing the old man's mind about offering the house to him, even though it was odd that he couldn't see the attic.

He would cross that bridge when he came to it.

~ Nineteen ~

SHE STOOD AT THE TOP of the stone steps leading to the snow-covered beach, watching him as he walked along the lake shore.

Irene wasn't sure what he was up to. Checking for icy spots? Looking out at the lake?

Wink had called Irene from the telephone at the station house and asked her to meet him on Edgewater Beach.

The afternoon sun was beginning to touch the lake, sprinkling gold glitter across its surface.

What was it about Edgewater? Why did it always feel so far away from everywhere else? Sometimes Irene wished there was a one-way bridge between Edgewater Beach and the rest of the world.

Sensing her presence on the ridge, Wink looked up at her from the beach below and squinted against the setting sun. Irene tucked her pant legs into her boots and descended the steps, joining him.

Irene closed her jacket and pulled the sleeves down over her mittens. She gripped her bag and continued toward the icy steps to the dock.

"It's time to go home. I have dinner waiting on the stove."

Wink grabbed Irene's hand before she could pull away. He wrapped his arms around her and lifted her.

He smiled and lowered her, slowly sliding her body until her boots touched the snow again.

The fragrance of the arctic breeze off the lake, the sound of birds overhead, was the perfect backdrop for his next words.

He grinned and pushed a stray strand of hair from her eyes.

"The Edgewater shore is unlike anywhere I have ever known. You won't find it anyplace else. And I've traveled all over the world." He smiled down at Irene and gave her a wink.

"This place has a rhythm to it; the ripple of the waves, the wind through the trees, the serenade of the birds. And it doesn't matter what time of year it is."

Irene met his gaze. "You really know how to have your way with a girl, don't you?"

Wink took her hands in his and spoke softly.

"I have something to show you."

~ Twenty ~

IRENE SMILED AT THE old man.

"I'm Elliott," he said, as he held his hand out to her.

"Irene," she said, meeting his eyes as she slipped her fingers into his.

He gave her a turnkey smile and kissed her hand; she got chills; but they were *warm chills.*

As Irene stood in the foyer, he smiled and asked her,

"Did you know you have a bright blue swirl in your right eye?"

Her eyes flickered with sudden intensity. She smiled and blushed. Her grandmother used to tell her that.

They moved on to the living room.

Wink was happy at Irene's reaction to the house. Each room seemed to brighten with her smile and laughter.

The man kept his eyes on Irene the whole time he led them around the house, with the same expectant look on his face. Wink did notice his attention, but he didn't let it bother him. He was growing fond of the old guy.

Wink found Irene in the kitchen. It was as if he had entered the elegance of the year 1915. He wondered if it had even been touched since then.

Irene looked around the kitchen.

It was nice, not huge, but it had a walk-in butler's pantry, which made it efficient. She walked past the nook, the dry, musty scent of old shelf paper filling her senses.

Irene wrinkled her nose and cast a nasty look at the ceiling.

The man's eyes instantly flicked back to hers.

"Cosmetic; plumbing leak. It was repaired last year – I will have the plaster redone this week."

He explained that the hardwood floors were all milled from trees that had been cleared from the property; oak, cherry, chestnut, and birch, and were decorated with ornate custom-crafted copper heat registers.

Wink was fascinated to learn that the main structure was 4 bricks deep, and that the bricks had been fired locally, at a nearby brickyard.

After an hour-long tour of the house, Wink caught a twinkle in Irene's eyes, and the decision was made.

"Sir, I would like to discuss the possibility of purchasing the property from you."

The old man turned to Irene and gestured to a hallway. He smiled.

"Make yourself comfortable in the library. We won't be long."

Irene peeled open the double doors and slipped into the room to wait for them to return. She drew in a deep breath.

Cherry pipe tobacco, old wood; and roses.

The room smelled like aging love letters, sprayed with the fragrance of the past. Along one wall was an old oak book case and another one, painted white.

She sank down into the weathered leather sofa.

And she waited.

It took less than fifteen minutes for the old man and Wink to come to an agreement on a purchase price for the house, taking into consideration the stipulations outlined in the estate of Captain John Stockton.

The old man had been the caretaker of the property since 1926; the year Captain Stockton died.

Prior to the 1930's, accurate records weren't always maintained, so the details surrounding his death were somewhat sketchy, but they were documented. The old man did his best to fill Wink in on what little he knew about Stockton.

The captain's billfold and his pocket watch had been found in his abandoned rowboat that had washed up on the Canadian shore of Lake Erie.

John had been distraught since the untimely death of his young wife, and he never got over the loss.

Speculation was that he had been drinking heavily the last night he was seen in Cleveland and he could have easily fallen overboard. He must not have been able to, or perhaps didn't want to return to the rowboat and the life he had ahead of him without the love of his life.

Captain Stockton had very specific details written into the legal agreement between the caretaker of his estate, if any, and a potential buyer that needed to be carefully met before time could march on for the old house.

~ Twenty-One ~

IT HAD ONLY BEEN a couple of days since Irene and Wink had moved into the house, when they received a registered letter via courier.

Wink opened the envelope and quickly called out to Irene.

"Aww, honey – Elliot passed away."

"What?" Her face appeared at the top of the staircase.

He placed the letter on the table by the door. "Mr. Hutchinson; the caretaker of Captain Stockton's estate. He died." Wink moved up two steps. He sat down and stared ahead.

Irene stepped down and sat next to him. She hooked her arm in his and leaned her head on his shoulder.

"I didn't know he wasn't well. He didn't seem ill; what happened?"

"The letter didn't give any details other than I need to be present, following the reading of the will, tomorrow morning."

Irene pulled back slightly and gave him a funny look.

"That's odd, isn't it?"

Wink shrugged and stood again.

"Probably has something to do with the fact that everything has been tied up with Captain Stockton's estate, since Elliot was the caretaker." He disappeared in the kitchen.

"And we just purchased the house from the estate."

FRANKLIN LAURENT, THE ATTORNEY, cleared his throat as he entered the room the following morning. He placed a briefcase on the desk and peered down at Wink, under his half-glasses. It was difficult to read his expression.

Wink nervously fidgeted in his chair, but he stopped when he caught himself.

"Elliott Hutchinson and my family go pretty far back. My father was a close friend of his and John Stockton's – did some painting at the house for the captain." He opened the brown leather case and pulled out a paper. "Of course, that was years ago; I was just a youngster." Forcing himself back to the present, he said,

"There is only one possession that Elliott did not donate to charity."

He handed the document to Wink and he continued.

"Evidently, there is a small storage locker at this address. The contents of the unit belong to the owner of the house; John Stockton's house."

Then he stared straight at Wink and corrected himself.

"Your house."

"What's in the locker?" Wink asked him.

Mr. Laurent packed up his briefcase and buckled the latch. "I don't know. I guess we will find out together, won't we?"

He gestured for Wink to follow him to the door. "I will meet you in the parking lot. Can you be there next Monday morning, at ten o'clock?"

"Yes sir, I'll be there."

~ Twenty-Two ~

THE ATTIC CORNERS were dark. A soft yellow glimmer of light trickled in through the cracks of the boards that masked the window.

Wink pried off the nails that had been driven into the wood, preventing the shutters from opening. Late afternoon sunlight quickly spilled into the dark attic, changing the mood of the room considerably. He made his way across the floor while Irene tried to open the attic window for some fresh air.

"This window sure is rickety. You're going to have to fix it so it doesn't fall apart."

Wink chuckled and backtracked to help her open it. She placed a wooden rod in the space to hold the window open, while he continued to explore.

At the far end of the attic, he came upon a door. He turned the knob and felt the door resist a moment, and then it gave way to reveal a room. Wink peered inside.

It was a small, musty space, maybe eight by ten feet, if that – awfully big to be a closet, but too small to be anything else.

As he walked further into the dark space, he heard the *slam* of a door behind him.

He tried to push the door back open, but it wouldn't budge. He groped around in the dark but there was no handle to be found.

With a gasp of exasperation, he realized that the door was locked.

Wink could hear Irene talking to him, but he couldn't make out what she was saying. He knocked on the door from the inside of the closet. "Can you open the door? I'm locked in."

Irene didn't hear him and she continued sweeping the floor.

He tapped, and then pounded rhythmically on the door. Irene jumped. He got her attention by pounding harder and he yelled.

"... IRENE ... OPEN ... THE ... DOOR!!"

She stopped sweeping and slowly turned toward the closet and she cautiously opened the door.

By the time Irene had it open, Wink had started to climb upward, bracing a foot on the frame, looking for another way out. She leaned into the dark, damp space and up at him.

Irene shook her head. "I can't believe you are playing games when we have so much work to do," she scolded him, mildly.

He jumped down and out and quickly closed the door. He studied the handle on the outside. Then he opened it and showed it to Irene from the inside. There wasn't even a place where a handle might have previously been.

"The window isn't the only thing in this attic that needs to be fixed. Can you believe there's no handle on the inside of the door to this little room?"

Wink made note that the floor of the attic had settled over time and that the floorboards pitched slightly downward, in the direction of the attic closet.

That could be a problem.

"There's got to be something I can use for a door stop." Wink wandered back into the closet. He winced as he heard the closet door bang behind him. Wink found himself locked in.

Again.

He knocked from inside the black hole. Irene smirked as she approached the locked door. She waited for his voice.

"Honey - Could you open the door?"

Smiling to herself, she hesitated and raised an eyebrow. He tapped, and then pounded rhythmically on the door harder.

"... OPEN ... THE ... DOOR!!"

The closet door opened slowly, revealing a grinning Irene. Wink pointed a finger at her as he quickly stepped out into the attic.

"Very funny."

He wedged a shard from a crumbling chimney brick under the door to hold it open. "This chimney could use a few new bricks, too. I'll call someone about it tomorrow."

Somewhere in the attic a beam settled. Irene jumped.

She cringed a little and looked at Wink. "Are you sorry we bought this place?"

"Absolutely not!" He winked and smiled at her.

Irene wandered back over to the open attic window and leaned into the screen. She lifted her head and wrinkled her nose.

"What is that smell?"

Wink inhaled and the fumes burned his nose.

"A fire … Something's on fire!" He jumped up and ran to the window. "And it's close." Wink grabbed his jacket and ran for the stairs. He bounced back in, just long enough to give Irene a kiss and he took flight down the stairs.

Wink jumped into his car and searched the sky. Irene watched his tail lights disappear down the street.

~ Twenty-Three ~

THERE WAS A BUILDING fire on the near west side; a storage company.

Wink pulled up next to the fire truck, immediately jumping in to help, running with the flattened hose.

After a few hours, Wink stood beside the truck and wiped his brow, relieved that, although it was still burning, the fire seemed to be contained, assisted by an evening rain.

Lieutenant Michael Carson walked over and stood next to him. He shook his head. "It almost looks like it was a lightning strike."

"I don't know, Mike; it looks like an electrical fire to me," Wink added.

"One of the last remaining storage buildings left around here. Some of the stuff in there dates back to before the turn of the century. I sure wish we had gotten here sooner; we might have been able to save more of the contents." Michael licked his parched lips and continued.

Without warning, Wink started for the building.

"Wait, Cunningham! You can't go in there!"

Wink ignored him. He kicked open the door and smoke poured out of the opening.

"Going in!" He stepped through the doorway and hit total darkness. Smoldering wood, waiting for a draft to reignite, cracked and hissed at him.

Above him, the ceiling groaned. It reeked of smoke and burnt wood. A sizzling board dropped in front of him. He stepped over it.

Rain poured in from the night sky, mixed in with water from the fire hoses. Parts of the building had disappeared like jagged black edges.

Carson was right. There was nothing else left to salvage. Anything worth saving was sitting in the waterlogged crates lined up along the back edge of the parking lot.

Wink walked along them, stooping to take inventory of what the department had been able to salvage. He placed his pencil behind his right ear. He tapped his finger on the clipboard and straightened back up. Wink smiled, his teeth white against his soot-covered face.

Among the crates was a storage locker that was stenciled with a name:

Stockton.

"I'll be right back. I have to make a telephone call." Wink said, walking backwards across the parking lot to his car.

FRANKLIN LAURENT PULLED IN just as the first fire truck was leaving the lot. The rain had tapered off to a fine mist.

The manager of the storage company joined them with a folder in one hand and a pry bar in the other one. He stooped down in front of the container marked *Stockton.* He attempted to pick it up, but reconsidered when he couldn't lift it easily.

"This one sure is heavy for such a little crate."

Wink held his breath as the top of the locker pulled up a little more with each twist of the pry bar. When the splintered lid was off completely, the manager stepped back and allowed Wink to reach into the crate.

Inside, he found a carefully wrapped, superb brass telescope – a work of art. Wink was fascinated with its age and function. It sure was a beauty. He hastily wrapped it back up in the cloth to revisit when there was more time to study it.

Underneath the telescope were stacks of old newspaper articles, layered in tissue paper and time.

And a leather-bound, extremely water-logged journal.

Mr. Laurent grinned as Wink signed the papers he had brought with him. They shook hands and made eye contact for one last time.

"Well, I guess there's no need to meet on Monday morning anymore, is there? My work here is done."

He winked and walked back to his waiting car.

~ Twenty-Four ~

"HOLY SMOKES – WHAT WAS THAT??"

A loud boom rattled the house for a full thirty seconds. Wink sat up straight as though someone had knocked the wind out of him. It was pitch black; he wasn't even sure where he was.

He had just come off working a week-long night shift and it was the first time he had slept the entire night in their new home.

Suddenly he realized he couldn't hear anything at all; he wondered if he had gone deaf. He looked over at Irene; she just turned over and continued to snore.

How did she sleep through that??

The alarm clock on the nightstand read 5:30 am.

Wink ran off to the window and flung open the sash. There wasn't anything out front. He rushed quickly down the stairs and bolted out the back door.

His eyes combed the yard, finally fixating on the lot next door. The house was a huge, castle-like Tudor, but neither Wink nor Irene had gotten the pleasure of meeting the man who lived there yet.

A shadowy figure hunched over in the center of the back yard. With all that crazy white hair, sticking out in all directions, the man had to be in his sixties – at least. Wink sprang into action, fearing that the old guy was in distress.

He approached him from behind. But when he got close enough to get a better look, he quickly turned and scrambled back to his own yard.

What the hell??

Luckily the man hadn't detected Wink, so he was able to hide behind a courtyard pillar without being noticed.

The old fellow pulled out something that looked like a broom and shoved dark powder into a large, cylinder-shaped contraption. If Wink hadn't known better, he would have sworn it was a cannon.

Thank God he didn't see any cannonballs – he was only firing blanks.

But if it *was* a cannon and he *did have cannonballs*, Wink had some questions that needed answers. He walked toward his neighbor's yard again and stood just outside the property line.

The old guy stopped what he was doing and stared at Wink. Wink asked him,

"Need any help with that?"

The man just continued to stare back at him. Wink tried again.

"I'm Wink, from next-door."

The fellow turned and went to the back door of his house, without a word.

Wink tried again. "Mind if I ask what you're doing out here so early this morning?"

The man opened the door and disappeared into his house. His back porch light went out and the house went dark.

"OH, WINK," IRENE SLEEPILY told him later when he woke her up to tell her what had happened, "He's just an old man; nothing to be worried about. You said he was just firing blanks."

"Yeah, *this* time." Wink frowned. "How can you explain a neighbor who fires gunpowder from an old cannon?"

Irene smiled sleepily as she turned back over.

"Artistic expression?"

Maybe she was right but, just the same, he was going to do some research on his next day off.

~ Twenty-Five ~

IRENE'S VOICE CALLED OUT. "Get that, would you, Wink?"

"Get what?"

"Somebody's at the door," Irene said, a little louder. "I'm washing my hair."

Tying the belt around his bathrobe, he ran down the stairs. Wink had slept in late after finding it hard to go back to sleep following the encounter with the man next door.

Between the pounding on the front door and the persistent ringing of the bell, he lost his balance and he stubbed his big toe trying to get to the door. The numbness quickly morphed into pain.

Shit!! *This better be good!*

"Hold your horses!" Wink shouted. He yanked open the front door and found himself staring at a woman.

From her appearance, Wink clocked her at about 65 years old.

Saggy under-chin gently moving, the woman stepped into the foyer without waiting to be invited inside. A few thin white tendrils of hair escaped from the tightly wound bun at the back of her head. A pink and yellow flowered apron draped over her head with ties that wrapped around her waist twice before forming a knot on her right hip. Although she was well-seasoned, he detected a certain femininity about her. She looked at his robe disapprovingly, wrinkled her nose and opened her mouth.

"Most folks around here get up before noon."

Wink glanced down at his robe and tightened the knot in his belt. "Didn't have a very restful sleep. I slept late this morning to make up for it."

Wink ran his hand through his hair. *God! Why am I making excuses to this lady I've never seen before?*

"I know – I saw you out there this morning." She walked up to him, her eyes at his chin level. "You didn't have the time to put on your robe before you went out?" She eyed him suspiciously, as if *he* was the one who was acting strange.

Good grief – were there *no* secrets on Edgecliff? Wink stepped back.

The woman's eyes arrowed over to him; she pushed past him and made a beeline for the kitchen.

Before long, she was opening cupboards and pulling food from the refrigerator. Wink would have stopped her, but he was so surprised by her boldness that he just stood there with his mouth hanging open.

The old woman ordered him, "Well, what are you waiting for? Grab a chair!"

Wink jumped. Once he had gotten over the initial shock, he obediently took a seat at the kitchen table.

Irene appeared in the doorway with her hair wrapped in a turban-shaped towel. She approached Wink at the table and elbowed him in the shoulder.

The lady dropped a glob of butter, then cracked a few eggs into a frying pan and flipped the gas on the Kenmore range. In a second pan, she carefully layered several strips of bacon. As she salted and peppered the concoction, Wink took advantage of the opportunity to gather some much-needed information.

He asked her, "Why does the man next-door have a cannon in his back yard?"

"Cannon?" She looked as though she had no idea what he was talking about. She sliced the bread into thick pieces, slathering them with butter and set them under the broiler. Then she raised her right hand and made a nonsensical gesture. "

"*That* old coot? Oh, he's pretty harmless – most of the time."

Most of the time? What was *that* supposed to mean?

She flipped the eggs over in the skillet and continued, "That's the *least* of his problems." She rummaged through another cupboard before turning to Irene. "Where are the juice glasses? They're *always* in *this* cabinet." She removed the toast from the oven and cut each slice into halves.

Irene got up and pointed to another cabinet, just to the left. The woman opened the cupboard and emptied it, moving the juice glasses to the first cabinet. Then she began clearing out the other cupboards.

"Oh, this is *all* wrong …" she said, her voice filled with exasperation.

Irene rolled her eyes and smiled over at Wink, speechless.

"I'm Wink, and this is Irene," he said with a twinkle in his eyes.

She was too busy to turn around, but they heard her say, "Petrie – Mrs. Petrie."

Wink was just about to say something that he might have regretted later, but before he could, Mrs. Petrie placed two plates in front of them at the table, each with perfectly round, sunny-side-up eggs, three slices of crisp bacon and a slice of toast, lightly buttered; just crunchy enough to let the butter sink into the top.

"Well, Mrs. Petrie," he said as she poured fresh squeezed orange juice into each glass, "it's nice to meet you." Wink bit into a piece of bacon as Irene sipped her orange juice.

Irene smiled at the old woman. "This orange juice tastes so much better than when I make it. What's your secret?"

Mrs. Petrie wiped her hands on her apron. She pointed to the upper cabinet. "The glasses were in the wrong cupboard." She turned and opened the screen door to leave.

"Aren't you having some?" Wink inquired in a voice filled with bewilderment.

She didn't answer – she just disappeared through the side door. Wink turned and looked across the breakfast table at Irene.

"What just happened?"

~ Twenty-Six ~

SHE SIGHED AS SHE soaked up the tiny lights glimmering against the indigo dusk along the shoreline of the lake. Irene couldn't help feeling so lucky to live in a place like Cleveland.

Dinner had been wonderful, but there was something extra-special about a drive along the lake road, Irene snuggled up tightly against Wink. It just made the anniversary celebration feel complete.

Well, *almost*.

Wink couldn't keep his thoughts off Irene and the other ways he would like to spend the evening celebrating their ten years together.

He got an idea. He grinned at her as they pulled into the driveway. "Wait here in the car. Close your eyes. I'll be right back."

"Another surprise?" she beamed and closed her eyes in anticipation.

Wink left the car running and quickly approached the side door to the kitchen. He placed his key in the lock and turned it. It was already unlocked.

They always locked the doors. He hesitated, and then looked around the kitchen. Everything looked fine to him; it was just an oversight – he would have a talk with Irene about it tomorrow.

Wink rummaged around in the crowded refrigerator and noticed three bottles of champagne.

That's a little strange; it's not like Irene to have champagne in the fridge – beer, yes, but champagne ... and three bottles?

He also spotted a hunk of cheese, wrapped in butcher's paper, with a small butter knife taped to the top. He grabbed it, along with a bottle of champagne. He kicked the refrigerator door closed just as he noted an open box of crackers on the kitchen table. They were quickly added to his collection.

Wink was very proud of himself. Irene would be impressed by his spontaneity.

As he left the kitchen, he paused to look around.

He thought Irene must have done extra shopping at the grocery store that afternoon. There seemed to be a lot more food than usual sitting out on the counter and table. And more beer than he'd ever seen in the house at any one time.

Wink shrugged; she knew what she was doing.

HE STOOD IN FRONT of the open car door with a blanket. His eyes looked upward to the window over the garage. He took Irene's hand and gave her a wink.

As he unlatched the door to the garage, he noticed one perfect red rose on the trellis; the only bloom that hadn't shriveled and dried up completely into a frozen oblivion. It was encased in a tomb of clear ice. Irene caught Wink's stare. She smiled at him sweetly and said,

"Roses are strong and resilient - like people. Some can overcome great odds."

They continued up the garage stairs to the attic.

Wink lit a fire in the fireplace, remarking about how it hadn't been cleaned yet. It went against his better judgment, being a fireman and all, but he knew how much Irene loved the ambiance of gentle firelight.

He had his back to her, talking, while his mind obsessed with how strikingly beautiful Irene looked in that simple black dress. Wink pivoted around as soon as the fire began its golden glow.

All of a sudden it was warm in the attic.

If he'd had tires, there would have been a screech that could have been heard for miles in all directions.

Months of staring at pin-up posters while he served in the Navy and 10 years of marriage could not, and did not prepare him adequately for what he found himself faced with when he turned around.

Wink was blindsided. He couldn't speak.

Irene had hastily attempted to pin up her hair, but much of it had already escaped in wisps that reached her collarbone.

She self-consciously fingered the long string of pearls he had given to her as an anniversary gift. His eyes moved up to her eyes, to her mouth, to the pearls draped over her bare breasts and continued downward.

To her stockings and what was holding those stockings up.

That was it. Nothing else.

When he didn't say anything, Irene gave him a disappointed pout and she scrambled for her dress, on the floor.

"Oh, no you don't," Wink said as he reached out and gently tackled her.

She loved the way he tilted her head back and took control. Electricity shot through her body. The instant he felt her surrender, he deepened the kiss, fitting his lips to hers. Irene gave into the hunger that Wink aroused in her.

He loved the way her body caught fire at his touch.

Wink leaned over her, fondling the string of pearls as they rested on her skin. Her eyes flicked open, and she saw a blazing intensity in his. And she melted.

WINK PULLED IRENE ON top of him, smiling at the sight of this woman he had just had red-hot sex with. He sighed as they lay, sprawled out in front of the fireplace, basking in the afterglow.

A knock and a muffled voice came from somewhere in the attic – inside the wall, startling them.

"Well, you guys might be content with staying here all night, but the rest of us are damn near starving to death!"

Wink stilled his caressing hand resting on Irene's breast.

He nearly jumped out of his skin.

They broke apart like teenagers that had been caught making out.

Guilty.

~ Twenty-Seven ~

IRENE SHRIEKED. She quickly clutched her dress and wrapped herself in the blanket, wide-eyed.

"Well, are you going to let us out or not?" the voice in the wall continued.

Great! I bought a place with a haunted carriage house.

Up until that point, Wink hadn't believed in ghosts.

He scrambled to put his trousers back on, tripping over his shoes, taking only the time to fasten his belt without zipping up his pants. He ran to the wall where the sounds were originating from.

The relentless banging and rattling persisted. He ran his hand along the wall and stopped about three feet from the closet door.

Irene's eyes swept across the room to the doorknob of the closet as it jangled incessantly. She froze.

Wink tiptoed to the door of the closet and grabbed the handle. He shook it back and forth.

After some finagling, Wink coaxed the lock to release.

He stood back and waited.

A familiar face from the fire station faded in from the closet as a young man, stepped out from the shadows.

Wink said nothing. He didn't need to.

Brian tried to disguise his 24 year-old smile as the explanation spilled out of his mouth. "We got this brilliant idea to throw you two a surprise party – you know; for your ten year anniversary."

Wink leaned against the wall and dragged his hand down his face, expressionless.

"You told us you were going out for dinner, so we figured we had plenty of time to get into the house and be ready when you got home. But before we could get much in the house, you showed back up, early."

"Then Chief got the *brilliant idea* to hide in the attic, and then we could all surprise you, after you got settled in."

"All?" Wink strained, looking around Brian to see who else was involved in the crime; who his accomplices were.

Irene, dressed in Wink's winter coat, slowly emerged from behind the half-wall by the stairwell and joined him. He placed his arm around her waist and felt a little grin fall across his face.

They watched as several shadowy, human forms sheepishly exited the closet, one-by-one, in a single file line. After all fourteen of them had assembled at the top of the stairs, the chief surveyed the scene.

Irene's silk stockings were strewn aside; Wink's boxers were barely hanging from the fireplace mantel.

"Then, when we heard you coming up the attic stairs, Chief said we didn't have a choice except to hide in the closet."

All eyes looked over in the chief's direction. He rolled his eyes, blushingly.

"And the door locked behind us."

Any other time, or if it had happened to somebody else, Wink would have thought immediately that it was funny. This took a little longer. For once, he was glad the door to the closet locked by itself.

"Well folks, we all gathered here for a celebration. Let's give these two the chance to get decent. There's a beer in the fridge with my name on it. Let's have that party!" The chief ushered the guests down the stairs and back into the house.

Wink and Irene stood silently alone in the attic. There were no words to describe what had just taken place. He shrugged his shoulders.

“They’re *your* friends." Irene smiled at Wink, reassuring him that he was not in the doghouse, as they descended the stairs on the way to their party.

He was just trying to figure out how they were going to explain it all to Mrs. Petrie in the morning. But, of course, it was none of her business and, she wouldn’t have any way of knowing what had happened.

He shook his head and laughed to himself, realizing that she probably would.

THE FOLLOWING MORNING, while Irene slept, Wink whistled as he headed out for his morning walk along the lake shore. But just steps before making the turn onto Edgecliff, his feet came to a screeching halt. The tune he had been whistling leaped back into his throat.

Staring up at him was a perfect, beautifully preserved red rose, peeking out from under the snow.

He stooped down and brushed the snow from its delicate petals. He smiled.

Irene was right; *Roses can be like people; and some do overcome great odds.*

~ Twenty-Eight ~

THE HOUSE STOOD THERE in front of him; overgrown yard, outdated fixtures, rooms that needed to be painted and papered filled with unopened boxes and packing crates. Wink was feeling more than a little overwhelmed.

He made his way deeper into the carriage house, weaving a path through mountains of antique furniture and assorted junk. Irene had gone to the grocers for her weekly Saturday afternoon shopping excursion.

Wink grabbed an old chair he thought they didn't need any more and took it outside.

Once he saw it in the sunlight, he reconsidered its fate. A few coats of paint, and it would be good as new. He rummaged around the garage, finally locating a paintbrush that actually had a few bristles left on it.

As he twisted the knob on the door to the garage, he thought he heard a high-pitched whistle. He heard it again. It was coming from across the street, by the park.

Wink took a walk to investigate. He smiled as he approached the crest of the hill.

There was a dog sitting in the grass, under a huge shade tree at the top of the ridge, facing the beach. He sat patiently, as if he was watching someone. As soon as the dog saw Wink, he leaped to his feet and raced toward him.

"Well, hello there, fella," Wink said, crouching down so he could get a better look at the Golden Retriever.

"And who might you be?" The dog immediately dropped to the ground and rolled onto his back, begging for a tummy rub. Wink obliged.

He smiled as the pup rolled back and forth with delight, and he chuckled.

"Well then; I guess I shouldn't be calling you *fella*, should I, *girl*?"

But the Retriever couldn't have cared less what Wink called her. She savored the moment.

The dog abruptly flipped back over and stood; almost on point, as if she had heard something.

Wink looked all around, straining his ears, but he didn't see or hear anything. Then, without warning, the dog bolted to the top of the steps leading down to the beach, and she stopped; and she watched.

"There you are!" a voice from behind Wink called out.

He turned and observed a boy, maybe ten or eleven years-old, wearing a ball cap, with a tousle of reddish-gold hair that stuck out in places, walking toward him. When the boy reached the cliff, he eyed Wink suspiciously, as if to be sizing him up.

But when he saw Wink's smile, he relaxed a little, and spoke.

"That's Clancy." He held up an empty leash and shrugged his shoulders. "She always finds a way to get out of our yard. We've tried everything."

Wink nodded and glanced over at the canine, still staring down at the beach, unaware that the boy had come to get her. He held out his hand to the boy.

"Hi. I'm Mr. Cunningham." Then he corrected himself. "But you can call me Wink. We just moved into the Hutchinson house."

The boy shook his hand and smiled. "I'm Dusty McBurney. I live on the next street over."

"What do you think Clancy's looking at?" Wink asked.

Dusty answered him. "I don't know. She's always liked to play on the beach. But lately she's been running away every chance she gets. And I always find her sitting here, staring – but there's never anything there." The two watched Clancy's head move from side to side, in silence.

What was she looking at?

As Wink continued talking to Dusty, he couldn't help sensing he'd seen him somewhere before. But before he could ask, the boy answered the question.

He sat in the grass and looked up at Wink. "I deliver the Press; the Cleveland Press."

Wink nodded. *Of course; the paper boy.* He found a spot on the ground and took a seat next to Dusty.

"What happened to *old man Hutchinson*?" Dusty asked him.

"Oh, I think he just got sick and he couldn't get better." Wink observed Dusty's facial language as the discussion about Elliott continued.

"Did you know Mr. Hutchinson very well?" Wink asked.

The boy shook his head slowly. "Not real good. But I liked him." Some of the kids were scared of him - thought he was a grump, but I never did."

Dusty took off his hat, placed the rolled-up leash in it, tilting his head slightly downward. "Aww, they were just spooked by him because he was old, that's all." He glanced over in the direction of the towering Tudor next to Wink's house and cocked his head a little. "Same thing with the *General*."

"And you're not afraid of old people?"

"Heck, no! The way I see it, I'm gonna be old someday, too. And I'm not afraid of me now; no reason to be afraid of me then either."

"How old are you, Dusty?"

He grinned at Wink and told him, "I just turned eleven."

This kid sure is wise beyond his eleven years.

"The man next door - why do you call him "the *General?"*

Dusty stood and walked toward the houses as he answered him. "My dad says he's a movie star. Well, he *used to be* a movie star." He kicked a stone across the street.

Wink asked him, "He sure doesn't like to talk much, does he?"

"Oh, the General doesn't talk."

Wink turned his head toward the boy. "I didn't know that."

"My father says that the General was a big star in silent movies. Everybody loved him."

"Silent movies?" Wink paused.

"You know – before movies talked."

"But how does that explain why *he* doesn't talk?"

"Nobody knows." Dusty put his hat on his head. "My father never heard him say anything … ever."

Clancy finally caught up with them. Dusty attached her leash and stopped for a moment to look up at Wink.

Wink offered his hand again. "Good to meet you, Dusty. I'm sure we'll be seeing each other a lot." Then he reached down and scratched Clancy behind her ears and smiled. "You too, Clancy."

"Bye, Mr. Cunningham – I mean *Wink.*"

Dusty turned and headed back down Edgecliff, Clancy taking the lead, and turned the corner.

~ Twenty-Nine ~

WITH A BASKET OF CLEAN laundry, Irene went from the foyer to the staircase.

She glanced up at the painting on the wall over her and she wondered why Kathleen had such a faraway look in her eyes.

Aunt Dolly thought it was odd that it still hung in such a prominent place in the house. So did Irene's mother.

"Her eyes don't follow us around the room, do they?" Dolly asked her the first time she saw it.

But Wink and Irene both loved the picture from the minute they each had seen it hanging on the wall, in its sculpted gilt frame, over the Mahogany lined staircase. So it stayed.

The artist had captured the beautiful young woman in such gentle, sweeping brush strokes, making it one of the most romantic things Irene had ever seen. It was radiant. Her attire was slightly more revealing than most were for that time period, but Kathleen carried it well, and there was no outward suggestiveness. Her smiling eyes gazed across the decades.

Each time Irene studied the picture, it looked as if it had been freshly painted. More than once, she had gone up to the portrait and touched the pendant around the woman's neck, half expecting her finger to come away wet with pastel oils.

"If you could only talk …" Irene sighed as she turned away from the picture.

A loud knock rapped on the door; she jumped and lost her grip on the basket, sending the towels, underwear and socks toppling down the stairs to the foyer.

"Oh, for Pete's Sake!" Irene jumped down the stairs to answer the door.

She opened it only to reveal an empty stoop staring back at her. She stepped out, expecting to see whoever had knocked, heading down the driveway. But there wasn't anybody – anywhere. Irene shrugged and turned around. She stepped back up on the threshold and stiffened. Her eyes dropped to the floor of the foyer and froze. Irene's body reacted with an involuntary case of the *heebie-jeebies*.

Sitting on the floor, staring up at her was a simple bud vase, with a perfect red rose. She wondered how Wink could have accomplished the feat without her seeing him. She shrugged and smiled at how much thought Wink must have put into doing that for her.

The door creaked loudly as she came back inside. She didn't recall *that* ever happening before.

Irene rubbed her arms, trying to chase the lingering goose bumps away. She took the vase into the kitchen, where she found a home for the flower on the window sill. Then, Irene picked up the laundry basket and continued up the stairs.

~ Thirty ~

WITH NEIGHBORHOODS STITCHED together like little nations within themselves, when it was all sewn together, the map of Cleveland looked like one big, cultural Crazy Quilt. That was one of the reasons he loved the city; her people – her diversity.

Wink made a trip downtown on Thursday morning and asked around about the original owner of the house – the captain.

Most everybody in Cleveland had heard of John Stockton, either by legend or reputation of his wealth.

But Wink didn't learn much more from the regulars about Stockton's life than he already knew, other than a few stories about his early career, from people in town; people on the 9th Street pier.

Born in Chicago, Illinois, Captain Stockton's first sailing was as a fireman on a river tugboat, out of Cleveland, in 1890.

In 1892, he was given command of his own tug, followed by a season engineering an excursion steamer that plied between Erie Street and Edgewater Park.

Shortly afterward he was promoted to another steamer, making him one of the youngest captains on the Great Lakes at the time.

The captain had never been shipwrecked, nor had he ever had a serious accident. His record was flawless.

Stockton was equally proficient as master or engineer of steam vessels, and knew the disposition of the passages from one end of the Great Lakes to the other better than anyone.

John Stockton appeared to have had quite an adventurous life as a mariner, but seemed to be best known by his work as the proprietor of a merchant ship; a 146 foot steamer that plied its trade to all 5 Great Lakes and beyond, rounding the British Isles on four occasions.

But a new, bittersweet story of the captain, who originally built the house in 1912, surfaced as Wink spoke to an older woman, who he found fishing off the pier. He hadn't encountered her on his previous visits, but she spoke to him, without turning around, as he walked past her.

"Such a lovely, yet tormented soul."

Wink stopped as she reeled in the line on her fishing pole. Seeing that she had snagged an old shoe, she laughed, and then tossed it back into the lake. She spoke again, still with her back to him. "He loved the sea - and the lake, you know." Then she spun around on her stool to face Wink through bright eyes framed in sparse eyebrows. "He referred to the water often as a woman who challenged him."

As she stood, a couple of giggling kids scampered past her, brushing her arm and she lost her balance, but Wink caught her.

"Hey!" Wink shouted at them, but they didn't look back. The woman smiled up at Wink in gratitude as he recovered her floppy, wide-brimmed hat off the walkway and placed it back on her head.

"Oh, they're just kids." She sighed deeply. "Tell me - why are good manners so hard to acquire yet so easy to lose?" Once she had regained her equilibrium, she picked up her fishing gear and they walked toward the shore.

"Did you know Captain Stockton?" Wink inquired.

She nodded and her eyes flashed at him. "What is your interest in a man who's been dead for almost thirty years?"

"Well, for starters, my wife and I bought the old Stockton house. We just moved in."

"The Edgecliff house?"

"You know the place?"

"Oh yes." She laughed, her eyes shined, wide with the memory. "I spent many a day there." Her smile faded. "But that was a long time ago."

Wink, hoping for more insight into the captain's life, continued to probe. "Can you tell me more about John Stockton?"

She gave him an upward glance, as if she didn't know if she should, but she liked his eyes – she always said that the eyes are the windows into the soul. So she began.

"In his day, John Stockton was considered to be among the wealthiest men in the area under the age of 45."

Wink stopped and leaned against the railing on the pier. "Was the house always in his family?"

She shook her head. "You're getting ahead of me. *Patience is a virtue*, young man." She set her basket on the deck and leaned over the edge of the fishing pier, reaching into a bucket, scattering tiny fragments of fish over the side, They observed as dozens of gulls magically appeared, gobbling them up as fast as they hit the water's surface.

"Sorry ma'am."

"The captain brought a young bride to Cleveland from Ireland. He designed and built a house that he felt worthy of her; one that flaunted his success." She lowered her voice. "The house was to be the setting for a large family; many children, and happy memories to last a lifetime." She offered the pail to Wink and he provided the birds overhead with course two of their dinner.

"Nothing but the very best went into the property," she went on.

Wink smiled. *Our property.*

"And that was not the only property John Stockton owned in Cleveland." She pointed. "There was a shipyard on the banks of the Cuyahoga River."

"The structure was built as a warehouse in the mid 1800's and sat vacant from 1880 to the early 1900's, until it was purchased in 1906 by the captain, and he converted it into a shipyard."

"Sounds like he sure was a legend," Wink added as the breeze began to pick up. "But how did *you* know Stockton?"

"Katie, his wife, and I were very close. A few years older than me, she was the sister I never had. From the day I moved into the house down the street from them, we were inseparable."

"So, you lived on Edgecliff too?" Wink asked her.

She nodded and caught the brim of her hat, just as it was about to take flight again. “Katie never cared that we were from different backgrounds. I was always equal in her eyes.”

The woman wiped a stray tear from her cheek. “When she became ill, I sat with her, night and day, until the end.” “It still feels like it was just yesterday.”

“When Katie succumbed and left us, everything changed.”

“I’m so sorry,” Wink rested his hand on her shoulder.

She continued. “Suddenly, where there had been laughter and music, there was none.”

“What about the captain? He must have been devastated.” Wink said.

“I was the one who had to tell him that Katie had died. He had just returned from an excursion – he had no idea that she was gone.”

“I will never forget the look on his face; the tears in his eyes. I think that was the night he really died.”

“What happened to him?”

“John was never the same after he lost Katie. We all tried to tell him it wasn’t his fault, but he was so overcome with grief – and guilt, that he never got over it.”

“He may have gone a little bit crazy. Oh, not in a dangerous way – he just started behaving differently. He began doing things that made no sense to the rest of us.”

“What kind of things?”

“Well, I guess the one that stands out in my mind was the time the captain had a crew of men come through the house and tear out all of the floors.”

“What?! Why did he do that?”

“We were never sure, but the rumor was that he was searching for something he had lost.”

“The floors in the house now are so beautiful; I would have never guessed.”

“The night after the floors were all replaced, refinished and polished, Captain Stockton took his rowboat out on the lake, and he never came back. I could tell he had been on a drinking tirade – I wish I had tried to stop him.”

“Something tells me that, even if you had tried to, you couldn’t have stopped him.”

"I suppose you're right. Anyway, they found his wallet and his watch in the boat. John Stockton never went anywhere without his compass, his watch and his wallet."

With a faraway look in her eyes, she added, "I don't think he wanted to go on with his life."

"Ma'am, you are welcome at our home any time." He touched her shoulder gently. "I mean it. I would love for you to meet my wife, Irene."

The woman smiled at Wink and picked up her basket. "I just might take you up on that invitation." As she walked away, she abruptly hesitated and turned back around for a moment and spoke again.

"There's something about that house." She winked and smiled at him. "You just have to believe."

The lake breeze picked up as the woman placed her floppy hat on her head, careful to keep one hand on top. She said one last thing before she faced the wind to continue on her way.

"Take good care of it and it will take good care of you."

~ Thirty-One ~

LATER THAT AFTERNOON, WINK and Irene hauled the old locker that had been in storage up to the attic for safekeeping. With all the activity around lately, there was no telling where it would have wound up, if it stayed in the garage.

After they got it upstairs, Wink and Irene began rummaging through the contents of the weathered old trunk as Wink filled her in on his conversation with the old woman on the pier. He also denied having anything to do with the rose that she had received a few days earlier, but she knew it had to have been him.

Irene unfolded the old newspaper articles and caught her breath out loud. Wink glanced over at her and asked,

"Are you okay?"

All of the articles were about the Captain and Kathleen, covering a period of about twenty years. She stopped when she came to a photograph of Captain Stockton.

"Gosh, he is *so handsome*," she gushed. Then she let out a little giggle when she realized she was swooning.

Wink dug deeper into the crate and carefully lifted out the journal; its edges that had been wet had almost dried out.

He flipped it open, beginning with the inside cover page. Irene winced and cringed as she heard the binding crack with the first page he flipped to.

The diary appeared to cover a span of at least two years. The first few pages centered on a voyage – the captain described taking delivery of a custom telescope, crafted in Italy.

Stockton had brought it home for his wife, Kathleen, so she wouldn't feel so alone. It was his way of helping her cope with being the wife of a mariner, explaining to her that a telescope not only helped him see things far away, it had taught him a valuable lesson.

The lesson was that, *sometimes you just have to find a way to look beyond yourself.* He reminded her that when she felt lonely, all she had to do was go to the attic window, look through the telescope and she would see the same stars he was seeing. And he promised her that she was never truly alone.

It was uncommon at that time for a man to show such a display of blind affection for his wife. But from the tone of the captain's diary entries, he realized that the relationship between a man and his wife was just that – between *them.*

Wink skimmed over a few pages, and then flipped to the middle of the book. As he began to read on, he froze; the words penned haunted him. His breath was shallow.

The entry revolved around a piece of fine jewelry, custom made by the best jeweler in Italy; something John Stockton had ordered 6 months before, on a previous voyage; the trip that he had purchased the telescope for Kathleen.

Wink cringed as the binding continued to crack with each turn of a page. He hastily flipped the pages to the last one, but Irene stopped him.

"You can't do that. It's so fragile. It should be treated with care." She smiled and added, "Besides, we have to start at the beginning."

Wink gave her a sideways look and reluctantly handed the diary over to Irene, who then carefully laid it out on the work bench to allow it to dry further.

They agreed it was a good idea to wait and only read the journal when they were together.

Wink had to admit that he was far more interested in the old telescope, wrapped in the cloth at the bottom of the crate. He burrowed through the rest of the old newspapers and carefully lifted the telescope out of the box.

Wink slowly unwrapped the brass and weathered leather telescope that had belonged to Captain John Stockton. He turned it over, repeatedly, with great care, until it revealed itself in its entirety.

Irene leaned down to slide the crate out of the way, but she quickly stood back up. It still had considerable weight to it. She grunted at a second failed attempt to make it move. There had to be something at the bottom of the carton – something they had missed.

"Honey, I think there's something else in here."

Wink stood and set the telescope on the floor, carefully padding it with the layers of cloth that had served as its cocoon for decades, to pick up the crate for Irene. "He smiled at her.

"That's a man's job. I'll take care of this."

Irene wasn't about to dignify or argue with his comment. She ignored his twisted male logic, and stepped back. Wink peered into the crate. Other than the crumpled newspapers, it looked empty to him. He bent down, gripped the side handles and hastily began to straighten up. He paused.

It sure looked like it was empty to him.

If she hadn't been worried that he might have hurt his back, Irene would have laughed at the look on his face; he had been so confident that the crate was empty, he wasn't prepared for the sudden resistance.

There was definitely something weighing it down. Wink looked inside again, and then studied the outside of the crate, following the resonances as he thumped on the sides. He jumped back to the interior of the box again and he placed his hand deep inside, searching for something.

There was a false floor on the bottom of the crate. The space beneath it was shallow, but it was there.

Wink grabbed a screwdriver from the workbench and began prying up the slats along the inner bottom of the crate until it peeled back. He reached in the cavity and grinned.

It was a tripod – the tripod that the telescope needed to be mounted on. He carefully lifted it out, opened it up and stood it by the window. It was difficult to contain his excitement, but he was silent. Irene asked,

"Is it part of the telescope?"

Wink nodded and added, "Without a tripod, the telescope would have to be hand-held." He gestured to the telescope, sitting on the floor. "Could you imagine how heavy that would be after holding it for a while?"

He studied the mounting bracket, and then he unwrapped the telescope, looking for the other half of the mount. It was there.

The beautiful mahogany tripod had features about it that clearly showed it was custom made for that particular telescope. Wink mounted and locked the telescope securely onto the tripod. Then he walked around to the eyepiece.

"What do you think it was used for? There's nothing to see here, except the city," Irene joined him, waiting for a turn to look through the viewfinder.

"This is in remarkable condition," Wink said in amazement. He extended the telescope and lifted it to his eye. "These lenses aren't even out of alignment." Wink remarked. "Everything stays in focus, regardless of which way I move them."

Wink stepped to the side and pushed the telescope over to face the window. He guided Irene to the eyepiece and adjusted a lens. He explained it all, as she gazed out across the street. Even with the dim light, she could make out shadows and a few boats, far out on the lake.

As she looked out over the water, she wondered what Kathleen was thinking each time she gazed through the eyepiece. Wink continued his explanation.

"A telescope like this has different lenses." He flipped the lens up and replaced it with a different one. "This one uses optics for viewing far away objects such as approaching ships."

Wink's voice turned into background noise as Irene became lost in the view through the telescope, far out across the rippling waves of Lake Erie. He ran his hand down one side of the brass cylinder until he hit a slight snag. He contorted himself so he could read the inscription on the bottom. It was engraved in copperplate writing:

Blackford & Imray - London.

Wink continued exploring the scope, in awe of the quality and detail that had gone into its creation.

It had an integral sun hood with sliding lens protectors, both front and rear.

Irene stood back and agreed with Wink. “It is a work of art, isn’t it?” But before Wink could comment, they were interrupted.

“What was that?” Irene flinched.

A strangled sound that might have been a sob – or a laugh – came from outside the closed door at the bottom of the attic stairs.

~ Thirty-Two ~

AS THEY CAUTIOUSLY MADE their way back down from the attic, they were met with an obstruction; a peculiar man who had barricaded the doorway.

Dressed in baggy overalls splattered with many different colors, the fellow was perched high on a ladder, holding a can in one hand and a wide brush in the other. Oddly enough, he appeared to be painting the trim around the door frame.

Wink stepped out around him and stared up.

"Who are you?"

The man leaped down from the third rung of the ladder and set the paint can on the driveway. Wink gauged him to be in his late fifties. He removed the beret that had been sitting crookedly on his head and attempted a partial bow.

"Allow me to introduce myself – I am Jacques; Jacques Laurent."

"Are you painting our garage?" Wink inquired.

"Forgive me, but …" he gestured frantically up at the carriage house and continued in a dialect that implied *French*, "but …I simply cannot tolerate this any longer; the color is all wrong … it lacks …" he smacked his lips together as he struggled for the right word. Then he grinned. "... *expression.*" And then he dipped his paintbrush in the half-empty can and climbed back up the ladder.

Irene leaned in and whispered to Wink,

"Did anybody say anything to you about the house having another caretaker?"

Wink stood at the base of the ladder and looked upward.

"You can't just go around painting peoples' houses without asking." The man ignored him. Wink raised his voice slightly and addressed the man again.

"Hey! Mr. Laurent!" The name recoiled back as quickly as it had rolled off his tongue.

Laurent ... Jacques? Could there be a connection between this guy and Franklin Laurent, the attorney who handled John Stockton's Estate?

Wink shielded his eyes from the setting sun and asked him,

"Do you know Franklin Laurent?"

The man suddenly stopped painting and glared down at Wink.

"Why do you ask this of me?" He quickly descended down the ladder back to the driveway. When he reached the bottom rung, he handed the paintbrush to Wink and the can to Irene. Jacques hastily trotted down the driveway, toward the street.

Wink shouted, "What about all this paint ... and the ladder?" Without turning, the man replied,

"I will be back for them later, after I have my supper."

Irene and Wink watched Jacques turn left at the end of the driveway, and past the General's house. Then to their surprise, he walked up the driveway of the very next house; a meticulous little cottage, with dark green shutters and a bold, red front door. He opened it, went inside and slammed it.

Another neighbor.

THAT EVENING, AFTER HE finished the last of the cookies, Wink reached into the fridge and grabbed the milk jug by the neck. He raised his eyebrows above the bottle as he drank out of it.

"Bad habit."

A projectile of milk shot across the kitchen as Wink recognized Mrs. Petrie's face peering at him through the screen of the open window.

In a heartbeat, she had her hand on the door handle and had joined him at the kitchen sink. He wiped the moustache from his upper lip with his sleeve, rolled his eyes and sheepishly returned the milk to the top shelf of the fridge. He grabbed a dishrag and quickly wiped the milk off the floor.

Mrs. Petrie patted his arm and grinned. "You remind me of my late husband, Martin– it took me a long time to break him of that nasty habit."

Wink noticed the smile lines around her eyes. It sure seemed to him that she must have been a happy person at some time in her life. He wondered how long it had been. She looked back at him as she hurried to the opposite side of the kitchen.

"Now, what would you like for supper?"

IT DIDN'T TAKE LONG for Wink to realize that these neighbors were a breed unto themselves.

Like one big, dysfunctional family, they were utterly obsessed, amazingly complicated and downright generous. They were completely *incomplete*.

And quite likely kooks.

This was certainly an unbelievable, nutty collection of characters. Wink chuckled at the irony of the situation:

A nosy old lady who sporadically makes uninvited appearances in their kitchen to cook meals for them, an eccentric wiry-white-haired guy who doesn't talk but fires off a cannon in the pre-dawn hours, and a peculiar, high-strung handyman who thinks he's some kind of Picasso.

And they all live in my neighborhood.

How lucky for me.

~ Thirty-Three ~

A GUST OFF THE lake swept in through the window, scattering the loose pages across the wooden floorboards.

She scrambled to retrieve them but she was too late. The breeze off the lake had other ideas.

"No!" she cried out, as she watched the journal come apart in the wind, each page sailing into a different direction.

She was gathering the worn and tattered pieces of the captain's life when Wink entered the room, in a panic.

"Irene – What's wrong?" He watched her chase the papers around the room. "I was in the garage and I heard you scream."

She stood and he saw the helpless look in her eyes. Wink helped her gather the pages together until they thought they had them all.

"What happened to the journal?" he asked her.

Irene shut the attic window and sat down, gently releasing the diary entries onto the floor. "The binding was so old and brittle, that it fell apart – and when the breeze came through the window … I know we agreed to only read it together, but …"

Wink sat on the floor next to her and smiled. "We'll put it back together. Don't worry; it will be as good as new.

It was turning out to be quite a daunting task. The pages were not numbered. The only way to get everything back in its proper order was to read each page and go from there.

Irene picked up a paper and began. She smiled.

"This must be the first page – Look – it's dated *May 22, 1925.*" She handed it to him.

Wink and Irene began to read the captain's journal, little by little, as they attempted to piece the pages back together in order.

Irene read, over his shoulder, the first page from the captain's journal.

The 22nd opened with a wet morning and a most awful sight.

We weren't far out, when the water began to gurgle. I wondered if it could be a whale surfacing beneath as the waters rose, tossing me into its churning depths, as the sea swallowed whole, everything in its path.

As I saw our sister ship listing over, you could not but realize she was a doomed vessel. There was nothing that we could do.

As irony would have it, the day ended up with a beautiful moonlight night.

Wink turned the page over to the back side to look at the next entry in the diary.

23 May 1925

By God's grace, we survived the previous day. Our sister ship did not. It was the last time I saw her before the sea consumed her. My wish is that these words will preserve her memory so that she and her crew will never be forgotten.

I must turn my thoughts – I will soon be on my way back to my wife with a gift to bring us closer.

Emotion tightened Irene's chest. She looked up at Wink and asked,

"What about their children?"

Wink flipped through a few more pages and then back to where he had left off. He breathed in and exhaled deeply.

"It doesn't look like they ever had any. I guess it just wasn't in the stars." He looked over at Irene's damp eyes, and then he set the loose pages back on the workbench. Wink stood.

"That's enough for tonight. It's late; you're tired, and I don't think reading any further right now is going to help you sleep tonight."

Irene gave him a look of disappointment.

"Can we read more later?" Wink took her hand and pulled her toward the attic door.

"Of course we can – just not tonight." He turned out the light and closed the door behind them.

~ Thirty-Four ~

27 May 1925

Nightfall is coming later, this time of year.

Sweet Katie, My wild, yet fragile, Irish Rose, I give you my solemn promise that at the end of this voyage, you will be my one and only, at last; as it should have always been. I finally see the error of my ways –

I have held this illicit mistress; the lure of the sea, the seduction of the Great Lakes, in my arms, far too long...

My heart will be yours and yours alone, from the moment I set foot on the Edgewater shore forward... My home and my heart lie with you, eternally.

How I long for the day when I hold our son or daughter; our two souls combined, against my heart. I can hardly contain the love I feel for the child as I pen this entry.

The stars in the midnight sky are strung together like the jewels that will soon be adorning my Katie's neck. Very soon, we will be lonely no more.

Irene opened her pocket for a tissue and clenched it in her hand before dabbing her eyes.

"It's just so sad."

It had been three days since they had been in the attic and Irene had insisted that they put the log back together as soon as they could. She felt a sense of obligation; maybe because she felt as though she owed it to Captain Stockton.

She brought a few more pages over to Wink. "I think there are still some missing. These are after the section that is gone." She began reading the top page to herself.

And then came the entry that made Irene's heart stop:

31 August 1925

The late afternoon skies are clear and blue at the first distant sighting of the port of Cleveland. It will be but a few hours now. The gift for the love of my life tucked tightly in my coat pocket, I can barely wait to dock before I disembark.

John Stockton was unaware that a new storm was stirring on the Edgewater shore. Irene's heartbeat sped up, then quickly skipped a couple beats - she knew what was coming next.

To their disappointment, the following pages were dated, in Stockton's handwriting, but had no words written on them – they were void of any thoughts.

The next paper in the stack with an entry on it was dated late September.

27 September 1925

I have not found myself emotionally able to continue this journal until this morning. I have had little to record and none of it is joyful, but alas, I must finish what I have begun.

At my last record, I was happy to see my dearest Kathleen; I could not wait to hold her in my arms. I walked briskly to the house, whistling, memories flooding over me; her laughing eyes, her smile, the way she whispered my name during the night while the moonlight streamed in through the lace curtains of the bedroom. I could see her in my mind.

But as I approached the house, I became fearful and overcome with uneasiness. Something was wrong. Horribly wrong.

The captain's handwriting on the page became impossible to read after that; the stained watermarks on the paper had discolored it, adding to its illegibility.

Wink sighed. He rested the last indecipherable page on the top of the pile, without a word, and he reached to turn out the light on his way out. Irene glared at him from across the attic.

"Not yet. I found another page from the end of September." She began skimming over it as she walked toward him. He inhaled deeply, and gave her a wink.

"Okay, but only this last page. It's past your bedtime." He sat back in the chair and pulled Irene onto his lap. He exhaled and smiled at her. They read the final page of September together.

30 September 1925

I do not know how much longer I can go on without my Irish Rose.

Not long ago, I was so filled with hope; with anticipation for the life we would lead, side by side.

Should I have known something was amiss? Might I have been able to nurse my Katie back to health, had I been the dutiful husband I fear I had not been?

And now, I stare at the symbol in my hand; the pendant that will never know the feel of her soft skin, her sweet fragrance and undying love for life itself.

I cannot bear the thought that she never knew the Compass Rose that was created for her alone– a symbol of my everlasting love and my promise that no matter where we are, we will always find each other – I with my own compass and she with hers.

I find it difficult to breathe without her smile, her laughter; her touch.

Did the love of my life die without knowing how much I treasured her?

Dear God – Did she die in pain? Did my rose wither all alone in the dark?

Irene shuddered at the thought. Her eyes filled with tears, knowing how heartbroken the captain must have been.

Wink, who had been reading along with her, turned Irene toward him and enfolded her in his arms. He was overcome with a sense of sadness too.

They stood. Wink clicked off the light and he guided Irene to the door to the stairwell.

It was such a very sad story. Wink couldn't imagine how grief-stricken this man must have been to have arrived home, so happy to finally be able to give his wife such a gift – and that he was so looking forward to telling her he would no longer be away from her.

Wink locked the attic door; his thoughts continued.

... and that gorgeous necklace - that she would never see. He inhaled deeply and exhaled.

Wink froze. *Hold on! How could that be?*

Isn't Kathleen wearing the pendant in the portrait on the wall?

~ Thirty-Five ~

"CLANCY! NO!!"

That guttural cry would haunt Wink the rest of his life. His heart pounded against his ribs as he stopped cutting the grass.

Screeching truck tires broke the lazy tranquility of the Sunday afternoon in June.

Weeds brushed Wink's legs as he ran, cutting a path to the street.

He vaulted over an old fence, broken by the weight of the roses that covered it.

The boy landed, arms-first, skidding on the pavement as he reached his dog, lying in the street. Dusty's stomach roiled; he pulled himself to a sitting position on the asphalt. Clancy managed to crawl toward him, just enough to collapse, her head in his lap.

"I'm here, girl."

She whimpered weakly. Dusty blinked back the tears that stung his eyelids.

The man jumped out of the pickup truck and ran toward them.

"I didn't mean to hit the dog – he just ran out in front of me!"

Wink knew he was right – when Clancy set her sights on that beach, she was oblivious to anything else that was going on around her. He assured the man.

"This isn't your fault. I'll take care of everything."

The man backed away slowly and returned to his truck. He shouted, "I'll come by tomorrow and see how he's doing. I am so sorry."

Wink squatted, then knelt next to the dog, holding out his hand. She allowed Wink to stroke her head.

Dusty choked back the lump in his throat. "How bad is Clancy hurt?"

Wink ran his hands over her soft coat, bringing a yelp when he touched her back legs.

Please don't let it be her back.

He had a soft spot for animals. In fact, sometimes he thought he liked dogs better than people. He clenched his teeth and forced a smile.

"Dusty, stay here. I will be right back." He began a backwards trot. "We're going to get her to the hospital," he reassured him, feeling his neck break into a sweat.

Wink disappeared into the house for a few minutes, and then he grabbed a board from the garage and carefully moved Clancy onto it, resting on her right side.

Together, they hoisted the board and Clancy into the back seat of his old Chevy. Dusty climbed in next to her.

The boy looked back up at Wink, helplessly, tears shimmering in his eyes. Wink closed the car door and leaned into the open window just as Dusty said,

"But it's Sunday."

He smiled weakly back at the boy. "I called the doctor. He is already on his way." Wink reached in through the window and scruffed up Dusty's hair.

"My job is to drive Clancy to the doctor. Your job is to hold the towel as tight as you can on her leg – and to keep her calm. Try to keep her as quiet as you can. Okay buddy?" He winked at him.

Dusty nodded and leaned over to adjust his grip on Clancy's leg. Wink jumped in and turned the key in the ignition of the old car.

The engine stuttered, then stalled amid a loud clanking and grinding noise that emanated from under the hood. He twisted the key again. And he held his breath.

Fortunately, this time the engine stayed on. Wink stepped on the gas and the car limped out into the street, black smoke misting from under the hood.

Time had been of the essence and, although the car did eventually do the job, he never wanted to experience that horrible, helpless feeling again.

It was settled; on his next day off, he was going to begin looking for a new car.

TWO HOURS HAD PASSED before the door from Dr. Fishburn's operating room opened. Wink wiped his forehead with a hand towel and looked around the waiting room. He spotted Dusty, sitting on the floor with his back against the wall.

Dusty glanced up at Wink with red-rimmed eyes and asked him,

"Is Clancy going to die?"

Wink inhaled deeply and sat on the waiting room floor beside him, the concrete cold and hard.

"Not if I have anything to say about it." Wink turned the boy to face him and smiled. He pulled a tiny brown bottle from his pocket and twisted off the cap, revealing a little stick attached to it. "Now let's have a look at those elbows. I asked Dr. Fishburn to give me this."

Dusty squeezed his eyes shut and held his breath while Wink painted his elbows with Mercurochrome.

"Ow! That burns!"

Startled at Dusty's reaction, Wink knocked the vile over, sending the defenseless bottle to the floor. He quickly scrambled to mop up the medicine with the towel, but it had already made its permanent mark.

He thought about how traumatic all of this must have been for that eleven-year-old boy to handle.

"The doctor is going to do everything he can to help her. Clancy is very lucky to have you for a friend."

He sniffled and met Wink's eyes, wrinkling his freckled nose.

"*Best* friend."

Wink choked back the lump in his own throat and stood, offering his hand to him. Dusty spoke.

"I said a prayer. Did you say a prayer for Clancy too?"

Wink smiled and nodded.

Just one? More like a dozen.

"C'mon, I'll take you home. Doctor Fishburn will call me when Clancy wakes up. And I will come get you."

He smiled, hoping and praying that she wouldn't disappoint either one of them.

~ Thirty-Six ~

That night, Wink and Irene read more of the captain's journal, carefully handling each page to minimize the chance of damaging them further than they already had been.

19 December 1925

My eyes are pinned on the lake, but I see no snow and ice nor do I feel the bitter cold. I am back – in the month of August. I fear melancholy is overtaking my daily existence.

Irene rummaged through the remaining loose papers on the table, but she stopped and glanced at Wink.

"There's nothing else here, until the following September."

"That's nine months!" Wink remarked, thumbing through the papers, turning each one over to inspect the back sides. There had to be more.

But if there *had* been something penned between December of 1925 and September, 1926, it wasn't in the attic.

Wink stood and gathered the papers together again. He skimmed over a few pages, then he brought them back over to Irene.

"Here, look at this one. I think it's the last page."

She followed the words, tracing them with her fingertips.

01 September 1926

The morning rain has moved on, but new clouds are gathering. Precipitation will be returning, and soon.

Barely a year has passed since my beloved Irish Rose wilted.

Today shall also mark the beginning of a new era – For today I will not be aboard The Compass Rose on her voyage across the Atlantic.

My crew will complete the voyage without me. However, I place my full confidence and faith in the competence and skill of Mr. Hale. Despite the absence of a digit on his hand, he is more than capable – a fine young lad who will fill my shoes on this trip.

And that was it. They had reached the end. Irene blew out a heavy sigh of frustration.

"But that *can't* be all of it! It's not the end of the story!!"

~ Thirty-Seven ~

Wink bounced out of bed, with excitement, early on Saturday morning. The time had arrived.

He had been experiencing problems with the Chevy Special Deluxe over the past year or so, which was to be expected for a car of that age. And he knew enough about automobiles that he was usually able to fix whatever was wrong.

For the most part, they had just been minor inconveniences that he handled with ease. But he just couldn't get that afternoon out of his mind – the day when he needed to get Clancy to the vet.

Wink's old jalopy had failed. And even though it did eventually start, he didn't know how long it would be before it might happen again.

What if he'd had an emergency with Irene? He shook the thought out of his head.

That had been the final straw. It was time for a new car.

Excitement rose in his chest like bubbles in champagne, as he sat on the edge of the bed, tying his shoelaces. Wink had been studying brochures and drooling in front of showroom windows for almost a week.

He was not an amateur when it came to buying cars; not by a longshot. Wink was the guy that everybody took along with them when they went shopping for automobiles. He seemed to possess endless knowledge when it came to what went on under the hood.

But Wink really lit up when it came to a car's appearance – the chrome detail, the head and tail lights and color. He opened the kitchen door and stepped onto the driveway.

Outside, the morning was beautiful; a sky filled with sunshine. The rainstorm from the night before had to have moved somewhere to the east, over Pennsylvania or New York by now.

Winston Cunningham may have been the no-nonsense guy when it came to helping everybody else get the best bargain at the dealership, but it was a different story when it came to himself. There was a vulnerability when it was about his own car; it had always been that way.

Wink walked along the outdoor lot, inspecting the inventory on hand, running his fingers along the fenders and bumpers. He dusted the hoods with his handkerchief, looking for flaws in the paint job. Any one of them would have sufficed, but it wasn't until he reached the entrance to the showroom from the lot, that he felt a connection.

"Who could wish for a handsomer sport model?"

Startled, Wink jumped as the feature car in the window grabbed him by the throat and refused to let him go. His heart skipped a beat. It was a 1955 red, two-tone Chevy Bel Aire.

"I like a man with impeccable taste."

"Sir?"

"You sure know it when you see something beautiful – but I'll bet you didn't know that she's also *good under the hood.*" The salesman dangled the keys to the car in front of Wink's nose as a temptation he knew he wouldn't be able to resist. "Wait right here; I'll get it out of the showroom so you can drive it."

Wink had never driven a car before that had responded so smoothly to his foot on the accelerator. He felt the engine whisper along the road with a quiet comfort unmatched by any coupe he'd ever driven.

"Feel that?" the salesman asked as Wink pulled out of the dealership lot on the test drive. "That's the Blue-Flame 125 Powerglide engine – optional, of course, but this one has it all."

Power steering, automatic seats and window controls further iced the cake for Wink. He was drowning fast.

"City or country driving or bumper-to-bumper; this baby fits the bill for all your driving needs."

When they got back to the dealership, all it took was one look under the hood – and it was a done deal.

He probably paid a little more than he should have, but Wink was so ecstatic about the purchase, that a hundred dollars didn't seem that important at the time.

He shook the salesman's hand as they sealed the deal and asked,

"When can I take her home?"

Wink returned about two hours later, proudly taking possession of the keys … and the car.

The Bel Aire seemed to take an instant liking to Winston Cunningham; she never resisted when he started her engine, purring effortlessly until he twisted the key to turn off the engine. Even when the salesman drove her from the showroom to the lot, she seemed to run a little ragged; but the moment Wink was behind the wheel, it was like night and day.

Wink waved as he pulled out of the lot, on his way home. He couldn't wait to see what Irene would do when she saw the car. He headed west, over the bridge, toward Edgewater.

With the windows down he caught the scent of the lake. He glanced away briefly and turned the engine off. He rang the doorbell – he wanted it to be a surprise to Irene.

The front door opened and Irene appeared. She looked surprised at what was sitting out in the driveway, but once she saw how contagious the light in Wink's eyes was, she found herself pulled into the moment too.

Irene walked down the driveway toward the new car.

He was there, opening her door before she could do it herself. She chuckled to herself as the thought crossed her mind that Wink didn't want her to touch the Bel Aire any more than she had to; a thought she quickly dismissed as they backed out on to the street.

~ Thirty-Eight ~

WOMEN BAFFLED AND exasperated Wink Cunningham – especially *his* woman. But lately, she had become moodier than usual. They sat at the breakfast table, in silence, until he couldn't take it anymore. He asked her what was wrong.

"Are you mad about something?"

She shook her head. "What makes you think I'm mad?"

Irene didn't want to admit the truth. She was jealous of the car. Even though she knew it was ridiculous, she was a little resentful of all the time he spent with it. If he wasn't washing it, he was waxing it, or insisting on taking her for long drives in it – whether she wanted to or not. She wished he was as eager to show *her* off as he was that *Bel Aire*.

Wink stood and extended what he thought was an olive branch. "Let's go for a drive. C'mon, I don't go to the station until this afternoon – there's plenty of time."

Irene glared at him. "I don't want to go for a drive." She stood and looked out the kitchen window.

"Okay, but tomorrow, let's look at the vacation brochures I left on the bed." He reached out and pulled her into an embrace. She did everything she could, but she couldn't stay mad at him. There was something about the man that she just couldn't resist. They both knew it.

He kissed her. Not the average, *good morning kiss,* but something else; something much deeper. Wink was really good at getting her thoughts out of the kitchen and up to the bedroom, no matter what time it was.

THAT AFTERNOON, WINK kissed the sleeping Irene as he folded the blanket in tightly around her before heading off to work.

~ Thirty-Nine ~

WINK TUCKED THE EMPTY thermos under his arm and hurried down the sidewalk toward the Bel Aire. He was glad he had a three-day weekend off coming. He loved being a fireman, but he really looked forward to spending time with Irene.

The Indian summer heat created an optical illusion-ripple in the pavement ahead as he wiped the sweat from his brow with his handkerchief. They had discussed using the time to do more repair work on the house, but Wink had decided to take Irene on a little holiday - some place that had air-conditioning.

He chuckled to himself as he realized in a week, it would be October and he would be missing this 90 degree weather.

He hastily stuffed the handkerchief in his pocket, but it sprang back out, landing on the sidewalk. He bent over to retrieve it, and quickly stood back up as he heard the tinkling of a little bell.

A man was walking into the hardware store in front of him.

It was always apparent from the front of the hardware store what season was approaching. Wink straightened up and found himself face-to-face with an early Christmas holiday display in the window.

As he stared at the display, he could see his reflection, standing next to it, almost as if he was part of the display itself.

Irene's favorite time of the year was the winter holiday season. For the past several years, she had lovingly decorated their tiny apartment as if it was Macy's Department store in New York. Wink smiled as he thought about how, this year, she would finally be able to have that big Christmas tree she had always dreamed of.

The little bell rang as Wink pushed the door open. He imagined the old man, or maybe the man with the tattoos on his arms that he usually saw, standing behind the counter.

But to his surprise, a young woman looked up from behind the cash register and gave him a big grin. She appeared to be sizing up the fireman in uniform as she approached.

Wink always loved that first inhale when he stepped into a hardware store – that cool, smoky blend of metal and oiled wood.

"Those Christmas lights in the window display are pretty impressive. Do you have more than what's in the window?"

The clerk went behind the counter that was scarred from years of tools and blades being dropped, flung and carved into its wooden surface. Wink read the name on her tag; Karen.

She reached under and pulled out a catalog. "They're brand new on the market. We don't carry them in the store yet, but I can order whatever you would like." She smiled up at him. "It takes about two weeks."

Wink nodded as she pushed the catalog across the counter toward him. He began flipping through the book, pausing for a moment at a full page, color photograph of a house completely decorated in strings of colorful globes. He continued on through the book.

And then he quickly flipped back again to the full color photo.

Wink pressed his lower lip against his upper teeth and slowly nodded. His eyes never blinked.

"You can take the catalog with you, if you want it," Karen said, with a smile.

Wink knew that, as much as he would love to take it home with him, somehow Irene would find it. That would spoil the whole surprise. He leaned over the counter at the clerk and in a voice just over a whisper, said,

"Can I see the price sheet for these?"

She handed him a paper. Wink's eyes widened as he read over the list. He grabbed a pencil from a can and leaned onto the counter, adding up the figures in front of him. He broke into a sweat. But then he pictured the look on Irene's face when she saw the house on Christmas Eve.

He supposed he could work some overtime hours over the next few months to pay for the lights.

"Well," Karen shifted her feet and with a flutter of her lashes, "is there anything else you would like to ask me?" Wink blushed – she had to be at least ten years younger than Irene. He hoped he hadn't given the young clerk the wrong impression.

Wink shook his head slowly. "I sure wish there was a way I could get these home without anybody seeing them," he said, with a half-smile. "I want this to be a big surprise."

This girl was gorgeous – the kind of gorgeous that belonged on a photo hanging on the wall of a 23-year-old bachelor's apartment.

Karen had to have known that heads turned when she walked into any room. Wink thought, Women always knew, but she moved with exceptional ease and purpose around the bins of hardware and displays, and met him, face-to-face.

"I can bring the shipments over to the station house for you, when they arrive, if that would help. Then, you could take your time getting them home."

Wink leaned against the counter and dragged his hand down his face, which quickly transformed into a smile.

"You know, I think that would work." He took the catalog and price sheet with him "I will be back in a couple days. Thanks, Karen – you are a doll." He winked at her and backed slowly toward the door. By the time he opened the door, he had the beginning of a plan in his head.

The bell tinkled above the door as he left the hardware store, although Wink didn't hear it over his excitement.

~ Forty ~

HE WOKE UP JUST in time to catch himself sliding off the chair onto the attic floor. He roused and raked his fingers through his hair, straining to keep his eyes open.

The extra hours of work Wink had been putting in over the past month and a half were beginning to take a toll on him. He was always tired and, when he managed to be in his own bed, he found it difficult to sleep.

He paused for a moment, confused, and then he reminded himself that he was there to set aside a storage and staging area for the light display. But where could he do all of that, without running the risk that Irene would discover it? That would ruin everything he had been working toward.

He dragged his exhausted carcass across the uneven floorboards, searching for the perfect hiding place. It had to be somewhere that Irene would be least likely to stumble upon "the plan." His feet transported him to the closet door, and they stopped. Wink rolled his eyes.

Oh no; I have no intention of going in ***there*** *again until that door is fixed.*

But, after a few moments of fiddling with the door handle himself, he gave up.

As he walked away from the closet, Wink wondered if Jacques did other handyman jobs besides painting. Maybe the old guy could use some extra cash. Wink liked to help people out when he could. He decided to ask him; and soon.

Then Wink noticed a small workbench in a far corner of the attic. He wondered if that might be the place to hide the lights. He walked over and sized it up – the space on the floor under the work bench looked just about the right size.

But first he was going to have to clear out the stuff that was already under the bench.

He knelt on the floor and began sliding boxes out. There wasn't much in any of them other than old tools and some nails and screws. But just behind the boxes, there was one more thing, covered by a small tarp.

Wink pulled off the cover and revealed what appeared to be an unfinished project on the floor.

He was not at all sure what it was supposed to be, but it looked like the captain just gave up and walked away.

Why would he do that?

Consisting of nothing more than scrap wood, little metal clips and strategically-placed plastic strips, he seriously considered throwing it away. But as he held it over the trash can, he pulled it back. He tilted it slightly to one side.

It looked a little bit like an uneven star to him. But why hadn't Stockton finished it? Wink held it up to the light.

Would this make a good star to hang on the house at Christmas?

He would have to rework it and wire in a string of lights, but he decided to give it a try. Wink smiled at the challenge; the idea of a star created through a collaboration of his idea and the original owner of the house that had been dead for nearly 30 years.

~ Forty-One ~

WINK WAS ALREADY glad he had taken the catalog home with him at the time he placed the order. He wanted to study the sizes, the colors and shapes of the lights, before they arrived.

They were at the firehouse, having lunch when the bell rang.

As usual, nobody wanted to answer the door. But when they got a look at who was on the other end of the doorbell, they all scrambled, climbing over each other to answer it.

It was Karen, the young clerk from the hardware store. She was carrying the first of several boxes.

He was ecstatic. This was validation that his plan was actually going to happen.

After the boxes were safely inside the building, they invited Karen to stay for lunch.

"It's just spaghetti, but why don't you join us?" Lieutenant Carson asked, escorting her into the dining area. When she walked into the room, they all stood.

Except for Brian Nelson, the rookie who was sitting on a stool at the counter, eating. He was starving and hadn't noticed the pretty visitor who was standing in the kitchen.

The chief cleared his throat and got Brian's attention.

“Nelson! What do you have to say for yourself?”

He rolled his eyes to the right to see what the fuss was all about. He froze; the fork still in his mouth.

When he slid off the stool, it was apparent that he was about Wink’s height, except with broader shoulders and a swell of blue-black curls, just unruly enough to add to his charm.

Brian was a muscular man, with warm, friendly eyes, the color of dark chocolate; eyes that could melt ice cream faster than any hot fudge sauce could.

Grinning, dimpled chin brimming with humor, his eyes actually passed over her and arrowed back.

“I like to live dangerously,” Brian said and pulled the stool out further. “Take a seat – I was holding it for somebody who looks a lot like you.”

She blushed and she sat down. And she smiled.

But not half as big a smile as the one plastered across Wink Cunningham’s face.

DUSTY GRINNED AS HE saw Wink through the windows to the firehouse garage.

Having earned the unofficial title of “Resident Mechanic,” Wink had spent a good portion of the past hour tinkering under the hood of Engine No. 7, but he discovered a new burst of energy when he got a break and began going through the boxes of lights that Karen had brought over.

When the bell over the door rang out again, Wink glanced up to see who was there. Standing in front of the door to the station was a boy wearing a blue shirt, with most of his reddish-gold hair hidden under a baseball cap.

It was Dusty. He stopped inside the door to let his eyes adjust from the bright late-afternoon sun.

“Hi Dusty. What brings you all the way down here?” Wink asked as he began counting the lights on the first string.

Dusty held up a bag and explained, “I needed a new light for my bike. My mom says the old one wasn’t bright enough.” He smiled at Wink as his eyes got wider. “Are you gonna put *those* on the station for Christmas?”

Wink grinned as he opened the next box. "Well kid, the plan is to put them on the outside of *my house.*" He placed the string of colored globes on the table in front of him and reached for the next carton. "I'm hoping I will be able to surprise Mrs. Cunningham."

"*You mean it's a secret?*"

Wink nodded and held the end of the string out to Dusty. "Here; take this and walk back as far as you can go – we need to untangle them and make sure all the bulbs light." He winked at the boy and explained, "If one doesn't light, they *all* go out."

"Do you need any help hanging them?" Dusty's question caught Wink off-guard. He stopped for a moment and studied the boy's face. His curious expression quickly turned into pleading eyes, staring up at Wink.

"Please? I'm real good at keeping secrets. Everybody tells me their secrets 'cause I never tell anybody. Heck, I never even told my mom that my dad …"

Wink held his hand out and stopped Dusty from blurting out a potentially embarrassing family indiscretion by covering Dusty's mouth – he didn't think he wanted to know the end of that story. Dusty closed his mouth, but continued looking up at Wink with piteous eyes.

Wink hesitated for only a moment before he tipped down the bill of Dusty's hat.

"Stop – Okay, okay. You sure know how to get your way, don't you, kid?"

But Dusty looked back up at Wink and spilled out the rest of his story. "Aww, it's been two years since my dad broke mom's favorite lamp. I bet she wouldn't be so mad now, if she found out."

Wink blew out a sigh of relief.

Disaster averted.

~ Forty-Two ~

"WHERE'VE YOU BEEN?" Irene asked, shrugging off her coat and draping it over the back of a kitchen chair. She walked over to the window and stared outside. She felt a cold draft.

"I thought we were going shopping."

Wink drew a blank. He looked at his watch; it was after 9 pm. Then he quickly blurted out, "Sorry - I had to work late."

Irene turned away from the window and she leaned back against the sink. She made no comment.

Irene went to bed alone.

STARS WERE STILL GLEAMING in the night sky when Irene opened her eyes and she heard the front door close.

As silent as a ghost, she sat up and peeked through the bedroom window curtain, just in time to see Wink back out of the driveway in the Bel Aire. She dropped the drape.

Irene dragged herself to the mirror. An older woman, ten pounds heavier than she was when she met Winston Cunningham, glared back at her. She stared at her reflection, wondering exactly when she had lost her looks.

She fled to the bathroom, splashed cool water on her face, then she smoothed her hair back.

Irene hated feeling sorry for herself. She forced the corners of her mouth into what she hoped would pass for a smile.

WINK APPROACHED THE DRIVEWAY after work. He had barely pulled in when he paused. Looking up at the attic window, he had an idea.

He hastily pulled back out of the driveway; then he straightened up and headed west on Edgecliff – but not for very far; only two houses down. Wink pulled into the driveway of the little cottage with the green shutters and the red door.

It was a perfect little French chocolate-box cottage. The path to the house from the driveway was made up of stones that shifted under his feet as Wink dodged the sleet to reach the front door. He rapped on the doorknocker.

His knock at the door was met by Jacques Laurent. He was dressed in overalls, similar to what Wink had seen him in before, but this time, there was a baggy shirt, with puffy sleeves over it.

That was the definition of a contradiction, if Wink had ever seen one.

"Hi Jacques. I don't know if you remember me …"

Jacques turned and walked back into the house, gesturing for Wink to come inside. "Of course I remember you."

Once in the house, Jacques led Wink through wide doorways, through mountains of clutter, until they came to a narrow flight of stairs. He was a little leery, but he followed and carefully ascended the steps. When he reached the landing, Jacques pointed to the space and spoke.

"This is where I live; where I work – where I express myself."

It was a studio – and what a studio it was! The space was wide open, a large room without walls, flooded with light from a huge window, framed in leaded glass panels.

"This I designed myself, in the year 1913; the year I arrived from Paris," he proudly boasted.

Wink could see how organized the man was, things arranged in order according to the color palette - the complete opposite from the rest of the house.

"Say, Jacques – I have some little repairs that need to be done around the house and I was wondering …"

Mr. Laurent turned toward Wink and said, "Continue …"

"Do you do anything around the house other than painting?"

Jacques began flinging open dozens of built-in cabinets, cupboards and drawers and began laughing uncontrollably from his core, as if the question amused him. Wink took a giant step backward, for his own safety. He couldn't tell whether the man was incredibly angry or extremely happy.

Wink thought about escaping down the stairs and fleeing the cottage to safety. But something about the expression on Jacques face told him it was okay.

He watched in silence as Jacques pulled out a blank white board from one cabinet; then a tall metal easel from the closet. After he placed the board on the easel, he repositioned it, facing it toward the window until the light hit it just the way he wanted it to. Then he disappeared.

Wink went around the easel and ran his hand over the board – it was canvas. He took a huge jump backwards when he heard Jacques open the door, returning to the scene.

The madman had a tray -- no, a palette with little splotches of paint on it. He rummaged through a cabinet, flinging brushes over his head behind him, stray bristles flying all over the room. He dashed to a drawer and rifled through it before finally settling on something suitable for his needs. He held it in the air, victoriously -- a narrow, long-handled fine brush.

"*Aha!* There you are, my elusive little friend!"

He began talking to Wink as he approached the easel and started dipping his brush, blending colors.

"Do I do anything other than paint?" And then he began his story.

"I am from Dijon, France, -- born in 1891, to be exact." He began dabbing the canvas with the brush. "I was studying in Paris just after the Great War -- this is where I met Adele; a beautiful American girl. She was the love of my life." Laurent paused and looked wistful for a moment, before continuing. "She worked in clay – oh the exquisite things she could do with her hands."

Wink felt himself blush at the thought. He had been leaning against the wall, but he quickly cleared off a chair and made himself comfortable.

"Oh, so, you're a *painter!"* he exclaimed as a wave of realization washed over him.

Jacques seemed confused by the comment. He tilted his head and, in his charming French accent, he inquired, "Why this should surprise you?"

"...I thought you were a *painter ...*" Then Wink reconsidered how he could explain what he meant, knowing that it wouldn't make any sense to the man. Or anybody else, for that matter.

"Never mind," Wink mused as he sat back in the chair. "Go on."

Jacques moved slightly to the left of the easel and quickly whisked a dry brush over the surface of the canvas. 'This, I call "staccato." He hesitated and walked around the easel to face Wink again. He narrowed his eyes at him.

"Do you believe in fate, Monsieur Cunningham?" But he didn't wait for an answer before continuing his saga. "I followed my Adele to America, and *poof* – I landed in this city of Cleveland."

"You were married?" Wink asked him.

Laurent nodded as he feverishly resumed working the canvas. "I worked as a laborer, and Adele sold pottery until the birth of our son."

"Franklin?" Wink sat up in the chair a little straighter, but Laurent ignored the question.

"This *un chalet* belonged to Captain Stockton. He was a great admirer of Adele's work." Jacques placed his finger and thumb together and kissed the junction. "A man of such great taste; and generosity. He allowed us to live here for a very small *paiement*."

"Captain Stockton seems to have had quite a mysterious life," Wink added.

"Ah, but don't we *all* have mystery in our lives? Perhaps this is what makes us unique." But Jacques sensed that Wink really wanted to know more about Stockton. And he liked Wink; so far, anyway. So he willingly extended the story beyond his own.

"Yes, the captain was a very mysterious man – except when it came to his Kathleen."

"You knew her?"

Jacques frowned at his canvas for a moment, obviously not pleased with what he was looking at but, once he grabbed a different brush, his arched brows began to relax again. He nodded and continued, "She was the epitome of beauty and grace, with the heart and soul of an angel. Kathleen was everything to him." He lowered his brush and peered around the side of the easel at Wink.

"The captain was a broken man after he returned home to find her no longer with us; he became very ... *how you say* ... absent-minded."

Wink found himself riveted to Jacques' every word – hanging on each pause.

"When he misplaced the Compass Rose pendant he had brought back from Europe for Katie, he became so enraged that he had all of the interior walls and floors in the house ripped out." Jacques bit his lower lip as if the very thought of that caused him great pain. "Oh, those beautifully hand-crafted floors ..."

"When he had the floors restored, I asked to oversee the crew."

Wink sat up straighter.

"As I began the task of restoring the foyer, it came to me that, possibly, we could inlay a Compass Rose into the design. I thought that perhaps it would be a wonderful tribute to the necklace and its significance." He dropped the paintbrush and he leaned over to pick it up. He continued.

"John Stockton was very pleased with my design on the floor. But in the midst of its creation, he invited me to join him in the library. It was there that the captain asked me to paint the Compass Rose." Wink straightened up and asked,

"*Paint* the Compass Rose?"

"Yes, he wanted to know if I would make an alteration to the beautiful portrait, hanging on the wall, of his wife."

"So, *you* painted the Compass Rose pendant into the picture, *after* Kathleen died."

Jacques nodded and continued painting from the front of the canvas. He smiled. "I did not wish to change such a beautiful work of art, but I soon realized that the captain would have *someone* do it, and because I knew Katie, I decided that I should be the one."

"Oh, he tried to pay me, but I refused. It was a labor of love."

Wink raised an eyebrow. "No kidding."

"As a gesture of gratitude, upon completion of my work on the portrait, Captain Stockton generously gave this little cottage to me."

"I will forever be in his debt."

"I am very protective of this little chalet *and* Captain Stockton's house – whatever needs to be done, I do it. So, if you need my assistance with repairs, I am happy to oblige."

"Is that why you were painting my garage?" Jacques winked at him.

Wink asked a few questions about Elliott Hutchinson, but he was repeatedly met with awkward silence, so he decided not to pursue it. He stood and held out his hand as he approached the easel.

"Well, I guess I'll be going. Jacques - it's been real nice talking to you. I'll let you know when I want to get started on the attic closet door." But Jacques was already on his way back down the stairs. Wink chuckled.

He started to follow Jacques, but he couldn't resist the temptation – he walked around to steal a quick peek at what Jacques had been working on all that time.

He caught his breath.

It was the perfect likeness of Wink, sitting in the chair. He was tickled because, while it was obviously Wink, Jacques' rendition portrayed him as a younger man. Upon further scrutiny, he noticed something else that the artist had added.

In Wink's hand was a weathered compass.

~ Forty-Three ~

IRENE UNLOCKED THE GARAGE and climbed the attic stairs, deciding to stay there until the journal was put back together – in the right order. She was in no hurry – Wink wouldn't be home for a few hours yet.

It wasn't until headlights shone into the attic window that she realized how late it was. She stood and frowned, seeing that there were still several pages that she hadn't been able to put back in place. She turned out the light and walked over to the window.

But before she could close the shutters, Irene's eyes were drawn to the street below. A car and its golden headlights paused at the curb, idling, just past the driveway. Irene was curious.

She stood at the window. Even with the swelling limbs of a towering oak next to the driveway, she had a clear view of the two out by the curb.

Through the window, she watched Wink unlock the garage door and flick on the lights. About a minute later, he waved the woman over to the door.

Irene couldn't watch anymore. Nausea turned her stomach, making her skin hot. She closed the shutters and turned away.

She waited fifteen minutes and descended the stairs to go back to the house.

TENSION SPIKED THE AIR the following morning. It was turning into that kind of week.

Wink jumped quickly when he saw Irene walk into the kitchen and stuffed his notes in his jacket pocket. Irene gave Wink a sterile kiss and they sat across from each other at the table.

She wondered if their marriage was coming apart. Did he think of her like a comfortable old blanket?

Lowering her voice, she said, "Why didn't you come to bed last night?"

"I was there."

"No you weren't." Irene shook her head. He couldn't have been there. She would have felt him. "You weren't there."

"I got up early."

"Wink," she lowered her voice. "You were not there."

"What *is* this?" he turned toward her and asked.

"You tell *me* what this is," she answered. "Why are you lying?"

Beads of sweat formed on Wink's forehead. "Good question. *Why* would I lie to you?" He felt it all coming apart fast.

"All I know is that you weren't there when I went to sleep and you weren't there when I woke up."

Wink was beginning to think he'd better come clean and tell Irene about his plan to surprise her on Christmas Eve. What good was the surprise if it was just going to make her mad?

Even though he had put so much money into this, never mind the investment of his time and energy, it just was not worth it.

"Irene …"

Without warning, Irene shifted gears. She stood and spoke as she walked from the kitchen. "Since you said you are working, I volunteered to help at the Children's' Home on Christmas Eve, if that's okay with you." She smiled over at him.

The sudden change in subject was Irene's way of smoothing over the rough spots that were becoming more frequent.

And although Wink wasn't completely convinced that everything was okay, it would suffice for now.

~ Forty-Four ~

SHE SAT BROODING, watching the activity from across the street.

He was partially obscured by the window display, but when he turned, she knew it was Winston. The young woman threw her arms around him. Then he held her hand up and gave her a kiss.

Later, when Wink got home, Irene waited for him to tell her what was happening to them. He didn't. Instead, he just read his magazine.

She said, "I went to the hardware store today."

Irene could have sworn Wink blushed and his eyes flashed knowingly at the mention of the hardware store, but maybe it was just her imagination.

"Why did you go to the hardware store?" he questioned her as he looked up.

She had to think fast. "Oh, I just needed a paintbrush."

Wink returned to his magazine.

Irene gave up trying to talk to him; his mind was obviously somewhere else.

An awkward hush fell over them while the snow continued falling outside the window. The silence was deafening – another invisible slap in the face. Irene's mind began to spin, imagining scenes between Wink and this woman.

He got up and headed to the door. He turned to Irene and said, "I'll be home in a little while. I'm only working a few extra hours tonight."

But it wasn't until much later that night that an exhausted Winston Cunningham returned home

~ Forty-Five ~

The General stared up at white clouds that were holding pink flecks of sunlight as they floated toward the water.

He shoved his gloves into his pockets and continued walking along the lake, eavesdropping on the music of the waves lapping at the Edgewater shore.

But he was only half-listening. He could hear a few Canadian Geese overhead, late stragglers on their way south, cutting a wide "V" in the sky over the beach and lake.

By the time the General got back to his house, the Edgewater sky had turned silver with tiny flickers of snowflakes racing each other to the ground.

Twilight was moving in slow shadows and he noticed a light in the front window at Mrs. Petrie's house. He crossed the street and passed the residence a little closer than he ordinarily did.

It was very unusual that Mrs. Petrie's front porch light was off with the door open. He walked past the house, then backtracked and climbed up her porch steps. He stopped in front of the open door.

She was standing just inside, clearly upset, the broom on the floor beside the shattered glass. Mrs. Petrie looked up and saw the General. He started to come in, but she stopped him.

"It's the dead of winter," she told him. "Not the best time for a visit."

In lieu of a greeting, he gently pushed past her, and let the door slam behind him.

With compassion in his eyes he picked up the broom to help her.

Wringing her hands, she fought back tears, which would have been an obvious admission of weakness, and she turned away from him.

"The police just left. Vandals broke in and ... I wasn't here. They ran when they heard me come home."

The floor of the foyer was littered with papers, books and broken picture frames that had been smashed on the floor, reduced to a fraction of what they had started out as.

The general gathered her books, which were scattered and splayed open, off the floor and placed them one-by-one, on the oak secretary, in the living room. He set the last one on the top of the stack, but quickly snatched it back when he read the cover. He stopped and stared at it.

The general shook his head as if he found it impossible to believe.

It was an album. Mrs. Petrie reached around him quickly and tried to grab it away from him, but he pulled it back, refusing to give it up.

"Give that to me!" she shouted. The general turned away from her and opened the book to the first page.

"You old coot! I said give that to me. It's MINE!!"

The general turned the pages. He had always been good about arranging and labeling photographs, but this was unlike anything even he could have accomplished.

His entire career in photos and old newspaper articles; it was all there, organized beautifully, right in front of his eyes. He placed it on the table.

Then he picked up a framed photo from the floor and slid his finger across the loose dust on its glass. He looked over at Julia Petrie, who had sat down on the steps.

A lot of blue moons had passed since Mrs. Petrie had seen the general's movies, back in the day. She stiffened, looked at him and bitterly said,

"There. Now you know – I was your biggest admirer; I saw all of your movies. I thought you were so …" She paused, not knowing what word to use. "… even after you turned into a bitter old man. Are you happy now?" She quickly stood and turned away. She continued to sweep the broken glass into a pile.

The general took the broom from her.

She thought she saw a flicker of a smile. The amusement in his eyes and the dimple in his cheek caught her by surprise. Her pulse raced and her face felt flushed.

Before she knew it, she was swept into the silent old coot's arms and they locked eyes. He lowered his face to hers.

The light above them in the living room began to flicker, and Julia felt like she was the 20 year-old co-star in one of his old silent films.

And then his lips touched hers. She melted.

His glasses were slightly askew when they pulled away. He smiled and, in a rough, gravelly voice, he said,

"How about a truce?"

She froze. "So, you *do* talk!" She turned away from him.

The General took her hand and pulled her back. "Or I could always kiss you again."

"What did you say?"

His eyes glittered back at hers. "I said I want to kiss you again, Julia."

She couldn't believe she was actually hearing his voice. It was hoarse and raspy, and just a little bit abrasive, but it was music to her ears. Her jaw dropped again and she gathered her composure. He studied her face and touched her cheek. She felt like a silly schoolgirl, without any idea what she was supposed to do next.

Her sudden shyness warmed him. She was not the callous old widow he was used to dealing with. The angles of her face softened slightly. He spoke again.

"Please tell me it's not too late. Let me help you."

She muttered something under her breath, and abruptly slapped his hand aside. Then she turned away.

"What do you know about caring … about anybody?" she sneered at him.

"More than you think I know."

She shot back. "You've been so absorbed in your own sorrows for so long, you don't know *anything*!" She suddenly felt old again.

It got very quiet.

He nodded and pushed his glasses up the bridge of his nose; then he took a deep breath before he spoke.

"I know you have been going to the clinic every week for the last two years, since about a month after your husband passed away." He touched her cheek. "And I know you are afraid."

A lone tear escaped and she quickly turned away.

Julia closed her eyes, her heart heavy with emptiness, and she whispered, "Howard, if you've come here to make peace, you got what you wanted. You can leave now."

The General turned away and slowly walked toward the door. He grasped the handle and the door opened in front of him. But just as he stepped out onto the landing, he heard Julia's soft voice as she fought the tears, calling him back.

"Please," her voice cracked and tears filled her eyes. "Don't hate me." He didn't turn around. "Maybe we can take care of each other."

"I deserve to be a lonely old man," Howard said, expressionless.

Julia did an about-face.

"What kind of an attitude is that?" She scoffed at him, in her best *Old Mrs. Petrie* voice. "That's just the kind of attitude that will make that very thought come true." Her voice was sharp and harsh.

He seemed to barely hear her. He ran his fingers through his unruly salt-and-peppered hair.

"Howard." Julia's voice softened and she extended her hand out to him.

She faced the window, watching the scenery outside. The snow sparkled in the light of the full moon. The breeze blew through the trees, creating shifting shadows on the lake.

The General joined her and took her hand. They shared a quiet smile. His voice broke the silence.

"All this time, my hopes and wishes have been for a much younger man; a different man," he said, in a voice just over a whisper.

"Perhaps a man I never was."

"Don't say that."

Howard's face looked blurred through the cloud of tears in her eyes. His gut-wrenching confession had rattled her to the core.

Howard cupped her cheek, holding his palm against her face.

"When talkies became all the rage, I had nowhere to go; nowhere but downhill, anyway." Howard sighed. "But now I am beginning to think that maybe it isn't too late for me."

A new radiance flickered in his eyes as he looked at Julia again.

"Perhaps I need someone to help me see past myself."

~ Forty-Six ~

CLANCY BURST OVER a snowbank and trotted ahead of Dusty up the driveway to the Cunningham house the minute she spotted Wink walking out from the garage.

It was hard to believe that this was the same Clancy that just six months ago lay lifeless in the street. Wink smiled at her zeal and energy.

Clancy had spent much of her time recuperating on the ridge overlooking Edgewater Beach, especially at nightfall. She could almost always be found on the stone steps leading to the park or studying the shore line from the crest of the ridge.

She dropped down in a jumble of golden snow-encrusted fur and waited for the belly rub.

Dusty dragged the sled past the General's Tudor and up to Wink's house.

The scraping of the blades on the bare spot in the driveway echoed in the vaulted silence of the late afternoon as Dusty pulled it into the driveway. He cringed.

Wink looked at the blanket-covered sled as Dusty hauled it over to the garage door, out of view from the house.

"Hi Dusty. What do you have there?"

Dusty peeled back a corner of the blanket and revealed several boxes of light strings, two boxes of spare bulbs, and a stack of pine two-by-fours – all tied together with twine and secured to the slats in the sled. A paper bag of miscellaneous hardware sat next to them on the sled. "Karen dropped these off after you left the station today. I think this might be all of it now."

"Is that you, Dusty?" Irene's head appeared at the side kitchen door. They jumped. Dusty quickly covered the sled with the blanket. Wink heaved the sled into the garage, through the side door.

"Dusty, can you get these up to the attic for me? I think I'd better go in the house and make sure she didn't see anything."

Dusty grinned. He was pleased to be a part of such a clandestine operation. "Sure can! Do you want me to sort everything out and organize it for you?"

Wink looked back at Dusty. "You know, that's a great idea! That would really help." He smiled. "Can you make a list of everything up there for me, so we know if we need anything else?"

Dusty's eyes lit up. "Yes sir - it's only a couple days before Christmas Eve. We don't have much time, do we?" Wink patted him on the back and headed to the kitchen door.

Dusty pulled the side door closed and began balancing the first group of boxes that were going upstairs. He opened the attic door and began the climb.

He heard a sound of the door at the bottom of the steps, flapping open and closed. He turned to the stairwell. Someone was coming up the stairs. Dusty walked over to the top step and he peered down the stairwell. There was nobody there.

He stepped farther away from the stairs. He hesitated for a moment, then shrugged, explaining it away with his imagination.

But then he heard the noise again – a whimper.

Dusty turned just in time to see Clancy standing at the bottom of the steps, just inside the doorway, big puppy-dog eyes begging to be invited along.

"Oh, alright, girl – c'mon. But you 'gotta promise you won't get into trouble, okay?"

Dusty was nearly knocked off-balance as Clancy sideswiped him on her way to the attic. Once up there, she skidded to a halt, all floppy ears and lolling tongue as she turned back toward Dusty.

~ Forty-Seven ~

THERE WAS A SOLID knock at the door.

She turned the lock and opened it slowly.

"Franklin."

His face showed no emotion. Just as quickly as it had come, the look of surprise on Adele's face vanished. "Would you like to come in?"

He nodded. "Mother." Franklin stepped into the tiny living room and looked around. "I heard you were back in Cleveland." He walked to the coffee table and picked up a small bronze statue – a sculpture of a man standing at an easel, brush in his hand. Clinging to the man's leg was a young boy. "How was Budapest? Or was it Rome, or Madrid this time?"

Adele was silent.

Franklin carefully placed the figurine back on the table, staring at it for a moment before speaking again. "I see you have kept a few of them."

She smiled wistfully, as if she was thinking about something lost to her a long time ago. "That one was always my favorite." She started for the kitchenette, at the back of the apartment.

"Can I make you some coffee?"

He shook his head. "No, but thank you anyway. I just came by for a minute, to see if you need anything. I'll be on my way now." He reached for the door knob, but he froze as he caught a sideways glimpse of the little bronze statue again. He whisked it off the table and stared down at it. Everything became clear to him.

Franklin abruptly turned to face Adele, with anger in his eyes. "Why couldn't you see that I spent my entire childhood like the little boy in this statue?? Always wishing … clinging to the hope that, instead of sending me off to boarding school every year, my mother or father …" he huffed as his blood pressure continued to rise, "… just ***one*** of you, would want me to be with you all the time?"

Her voice was beginning to show signs of emotion. "I am very proud of you, Franklin; you have such a successful career. You are everything I hoped you to be … everything I couldn't be."

"It's all about decisions – choices, isn't it Mother? It's true, I have a promising career at the firm." He sat in the chair, across from her.

"Did it ever occur to either of you that I would have made different choices? But I was never given the chance to decide anything for myself."

She swallowed hard. "Franklin, you are not the only one whose decisions were made for you," Then, with more emotion in her voice; a distant sadness, their eyes met and she continued.

"My father; your grandfather, was a very strong-willed man. He always got what he wanted." She sighed.

"I used to wish I'd had the opportunity to meet him, you know," he added.

"When I was a young girl, I fell hopelessly in love with a boy. He was literally, the boy down the street."

Franklin shifted, uncomfortably, in the chair.

"My father didn't like him; his family wasn't good enough, he didn't have any money. He even hated his name." Adele stood and walked to the window. She turned away from him.

"Anyway, Jeffrey and I were planning to elope – that means we were getting married."

"Mother, I know what it means." He listened intently; rigid.

"But my father found out somehow and sent me away for the summer to live with my grandmother. And when I came back home, I discovered that Jeffrey had joined the Navy and had gone overseas."

"And you didn't know this before you left town?"

Adele looked at the floor and shook her head.

Light poured in through the window. Adele moved and stopped in front of the panes. She faced her son. Her shadow cut the light in half as she weakly told him, "My father told him I had gotten married."

Franklin observed his mother from across the room. She'd had many faces in his eyes before, most of them he'd held little regard for, but the face she was wearing now was unlike anything he'd seen before – pain.

"Jeffrey was killed a month after I arrived home, when the submarine he was on board was torpedoed."

"That must have been difficult for you."

She turned away and spoke again. "Grief doesn't always appear in the moment of loss. Sometimes the heartache comes in the quiet of the aftermath."

Franklin asked her, "What did you do?"

She inhaled deeply. "My father sent me to Paris for a year, where I enrolled in art classes. And that's when I met Jacques Laurent."

Franklin let out a sigh of aversion.

"Don't be so hard on your father. He's a good man. I never gave him much to work with." She let out a nervous exhale.

"I went to Europe for two reasons. One was to lose myself in art. The second reason was far more important to me at the time – I never forgave my father. I vowed that I would do everything I could to defy his wishes; I set out to find a man as close to Jeffrey as possible."

"I think I tried too hard to make Jacques be like Jeffrey. And he was not very happy about that. Nothing he did could please me – and Lord, he tried with everything he had in him."

"But he wasn't Jeffrey." She inhaled and exhaled deeply.

"It took a while, I will be honest with you, but I learned to love your father for who he was. And then you came along. We were very happy; for awhile anyway. There was never a child born into this world that was wanted and loved any more than Franklin Laurent." She smiled weakly at him. "But eventually, even that wasn't enough to keep us together."

"If I learned one valuable life lesson, it was this: "People are not like clay – you can't always smoosh them into what you want them to be."

Franklin smiled. "*Smoosh.*" He let out a little chuckle. "Mother - you always did have a way with words."

Adele looked over at him and, in a broken voice, asked, "How is your father?"

"Mother - I rarely have the time to stop and visit with him, and when I do, we have nothing to talk about. What about you? Have you tried to see him?"

"Oh, Franklin, it's been so many years now. I am sure that he doesn't want to see me."

He walked up to Adele and met her, eye-to-eye. "*Now* who's making decisions for others without asking first?" He opened the door. But before he got out, Adele ran to him and they shared a long-overdue hug.

"I hope you will join Nora and me for Christmas dinner. After all, it will be the last Christmas with only the two of us; next year we will be three."

"Will Jacques be there?" she asked.

"Maybe. I had Nora ask him – he likes her."

As she leaned against the closed door, Adele suddenly realized what Franklin was trying to tell her.

Three?

She was going to be a grandmother.

~ Forty-Eight ~

CLANCY HAD FINISHED exploring the attic and joined Dusty at the window. Recognizing the familiar scene outside, she jumped up, onto the window frame, with a sense of proprietorship.

Dusty rearranged the boxes Wink had on the floor, to make room for the rest of them, but as he slid a small box with his foot, it turned over, spilling its contents out on the floor.

He started to pick up the pieces, but was surprised to find that they were all attached to each other by cloth-covered wire and little metal clips. As Dusty held the first one up to the light, he could see that it was no accident that they were strung together. Surprise flashed in his eyes.

He smiled and bent down with his hands on his knees. Still inside the box was a chunk of wood and several plastic strips.

The star for the house – the one that the captain started; I bet this is it! Wink had shared his idea for the star with him, only a week before.

Dusty set the flashlight on the floor and crawled along the wall, searching for a metal clip that had sprung loose from the string as he had pulled it out of the box.

A cold draft seeped through the cracks along the old window frame. Although most of the windows on the property were suffering from various degrees of wear and moisture, this particular window had been neglected, being in the attic, which was rarely visited.

Hiding the lights in the attic closet for Wink had become a challenge for Dusty. Not only was it important to him to keep it a secret from Mrs. Cunningham, he was intrigued as to the art behind the whole process. They had spent hours discussing the plan. Possessing a scientific mind well beyond his years, he couldn't wait to implement the display with Wink.

Clancy jumped up, bracing her front paws on the weathered, old wooden window frame, to see what Dusty was looking at.

Dusty's cheeks flushed as he watched the bottom of the frame separate with Clancy's zealous attempt to join the party. He quickly pulled her back.

"Clancy, you're not even supposed to be up here, girl. Be careful."

He kneeled beside the broken frame and pressed the joint back together, but it just popped apart again. He pushed hard, a second time, placing his palms downward, using his weight as he stood back up.

But his weight was too much for the old window frame. The right corner broke completely off.

Dusty tried to patch the broken piece back, but he stopped when he noticed a small cavity in the wall, just beneath the frame. He knocked on the plaster wall and noticed that the closer he got to the floor under the window, the sound changed. It was hollow.

He shined the flashlight down the hole under the frame.

Dusty leaned in, curiously peering into the gaping hole. He observed a shimmering flicker of gold.

Upon further scrutiny, he saw that there appeared to be a delicate chain wedged in the open space between the frame and the plaster lathe wall.

He reached in and was hit with a stunning revelation. Clancy wagged her tail and then she sat down next to him. Her reddish-gold locks settled.

And Dusty's stood on end.

He gulped as he held it up to the light. *A necklace.*

There were no identifiable marks on the piece; nothing that would indicate who it belonged to, but Dusty slipped it into his pants pocket, so he could give it to Wink in the morning.

Wait! The Compass Rose; the one in the portrait that was on the wall over the stairs. The pendant that Captain Stockton lost almost 30 years ago ... ***this is it!***

His expression fell. This was incredibly draining information for an eleven year-old to comprehend. He rested his head in his hands.

Dusty was beginning to realize that he was no ordinary eleven year-old.

~ Forty-Nine ~

THE YOUNG WOMAN WAS inside the hardware store with Wink. Irene observed as they engaged in deep conversation. She couldn't watch anymore. She ran to the car and pulled away as fast as she could.

After Wink got home, they were about to walk out the door to run some holiday errands, when the telephone rang and Wink jumped back into the kitchen to answer it. Irene peeked into the kitchen, with an inquisitive look.

He covered the mouthpiece on the receiver and said to her, "I'm ready. Why don't you wait for me out in the car? I'll be right there."

When Wink climbed into the Bel Aire, Irene greeted his grin with a weak, damp-eyed smile.

Outside the department store, Wink asked her if she wanted to go to a movie downtown. She told him no.

Disappointed, he turned away from her, stone-faced and walked away.

When they pulled into the driveway, he turned back to her and said, "I have to work late again tomorrow night."

Of course he does.

An awkward silence fell over them while the snow continued.

She stared at his back when he turned away, wishing she had something to throw at him.

Irene went to bed early. She woke up around eleven o'clock that night. Wink reached for Irene in his sleep, but she shrank back from him.

He woke up. "Whatever it is, I wish you would talk to me about it."

"Everything's fine. Good night." Irene turned away from him before she could see how much that had hurt him. She lay in the dark, trying to clear unhappy thoughts from her mind.

Wink had sensed a shift in their relationship. He couldn't pinpoint it, but something was different. They were fighting more than they ever had.

The blue spark in her eyes had dimmed and, with only two days until Christmas, he didn't know how to make things better.

After he had fallen back asleep, Irene dropped her feet to the floor and stood, her face lost in the shadows.

It was over.

Maybe not completely over, but finished enough that she knew what she had to do. Irene went downstairs. She left the lights off and went into the living room, curled up on the sofa and fell asleep.

Her decision had been made.

~ Fifty ~

SUNLIGHT ROLLED ACROSS THE lake shore, the clouds so thick when daylight finally dawned, it was impossible to see the water from the street.

The Bel Aire reluctantly started for Irene, but it refused to shift into reverse; just another reminder of how much she resented the car.

It was impossible to leave the garage. She banged the steering wheel with one hand. "Stupid Chevy! *You owe me!!"*

Leaving the car still running, she jumped out in frustration and she slammed the door shut as hard as she could.

"I ***hate*** *you!"*

At the harshness of those words, without warning, it became deafeningly silent in the garage as the Bel Aire sputtered, and stalled.

Then, from somewhere under the hood, a tiny whine faded into a faint, pitiful whistling cry as Irene pulled the garage door down and locked it. She sniffed hard, wiped her eyes, unlocked the door to the kitchen and went inside.

BUTTERFLIES TOOK FLIGHT IN her stomach, as Irene paced up and down the driveway, waiting for the taxi to take her to the bus station.

Clancy loped up from behind and shoved her muzzle up to Irene's hand as she walked, forcing her to pat her head. Irene rested and kneeled in the snow to rub her velvety ears and bury her face in the dog's neck. Clancy was an affectionate dog who seemed to sense when things were out-of-sorts in peoples' lives.

Irene stood again and returned to the front of the house. She turned to Clancy, who was still in the driveway, staring back at her.

"It's okay, girl. I'm fine. You can go play – really, you can." Clancy gave her a look that said she really didn't believe her, but after a minute, she bounded down the street to the stairs leading to the beach.

Irene stepped back up on the front stoop, and she sat next to her little brown suitcase.

On his way to fetch Clancy again, Dusty appeared from around the corner as he approached the stretch of houses heading to the park. No surprise to him, he spotted Clancy in her usual watching place – facing the lake on the cliff overhanging Edgewater Beach.

But as he passed the Cunningham house Dusty noticed Irene, waiting outside on the front step. He crossed the yard and up the driveway; he could see that Mrs. Cunningham had been crying. Something was wrong.

She looked up at Dusty, shielding her eyes against the wind. His hair looked more of a bronzed brown with sandy ends in the pre-blizzard late morning light.

She turned away and began sweeping the tiny flakes of snow off her suitcase. "I saw Clancy a few minutes ago – she was heading off to the beach. You'd better take her back home before the blizzard sets in."

But Dusty didn't hear anything she said. He asked, "Are you going shopping?"

Staring into the falling snow, she said "Oh, I decided to visit my cousin in Pittsburgh."

Why would she leave the day before Christmas?

Irene rose from the step as the cab appeared in the driveway. She began walking down the drive alone, but Dusty fell into step, alongside her.

He walked to the taxi with her, in silence. The driver put her suitcase in the trunk and opened the door for her. She smiled weakly at Dusty and got into the cab.

But she hastily backed out; she reached in her pocket and handed him an envelope. “Dusty, I want you to give this to Mr. Cunningham for me.” Her lips quivered.

She touched his cheek with her hand and smiled faintly at him as she got back into the cab. He blinked at her.

“Merry Christmas, Dusty.”

As the taxi made its way down Edgecliff to the corner, Irene stared out the window, wondering how this could be the same street she and Wink had driven down for the first time, less than a year ago, filled with hope and anticipation for their future.

~ Fifty-One ~

A HALF-HEARTED SNOW had begun to fall, as if it wasn't sure if it really wanted to or not.

His hands stung with the cold as he studied the envelope Mrs. Cunningham had given him. He had a bad feeling about it; she seemed so sad when she gave it to him.

He turned it over.

Dusty's father always said that you shouldn't meddle in other peoples' business. He was usually right. He stuffed the envelope in his jacket pocket.

They were such nice people; the Cunninghams.

But before he turned away, he noticed that the side door to the garage was standing open. Wink must have been in there earlier that morning before he went to work, and forgot to close it.

As he approached, he heard a sound – a jangling coming from the back of the garage. He heard it again. Dusty followed the sound until he found himself standing beside the Bel Aire.

There it was again. He opened the car door. The keys were jingling in the ignition.

Dusty reached in to pull the keys from the dashboard, but he was met with a tingling in his hand. It startled him and he lurched forward, causing the envelope to fall from his pocket.

The glue on the seal of the envelope had gotten wet enough to render it useless and the paper peeked out from the top. It didn't take much encouragement for the words along the fold to jump out at him.

"Sorry, Dad, but I just 'gotta do this." He unfolded it the rest of the way and continued to read.

Dusty's heart stilled.

All he needed to see was the part where Irene told Wink she was leaving. And that she thought he didn't care about her anymore. He jammed the letter back into the envelope.

He heard the jingling again. The keys.

Dusty looked back at the open side door to the garage – there was no wind. He walked slowly around to the front of the Bel Aire.

Just as he started back to the garage door, he saw his own shadow as he was hit from behind with a bright flash that ceased as quickly as it had appeared. He turned back to face the car.

The headlights flashed on and off again. He jumped back five feet.

Dusty considered himself to be pretty brave, for an eleven-year-old, but this was creepy, even for him. He slowly inched back and touched the front driver's side fender.

The engine fired up and the headlights flashed on – high-beam.

And this time they stayed on.

The side door to the garage was open, but Dusty knew that you were never supposed to run a car in a closed garage – that could be deadly. He quickly ran and strained to lift the heavy front garage door.

He grunted as his hands struggled to pull up on the metal handles at the center of the base. It was no use; he was an eleven year old kid. He backed away from the door; his shoulders sagged.

Consternation rose in Dusty's throat, but something deep within him made him try one last time.

The door groaned and creaked in protest, the springs trying as hard as they could to do their job. Then the door separated from the concrete floor. And it rose with no effort.

Dusty jumped as he heard the engine rev a few times, stronger with each one.

Is the car out of control?

He put on his earmuffs and gloves, grabbed the driver's door and jumped into the Chevy, out of self-defense. What would happen if the car went out into the street with nobody in it? How many people could be hurt … or even worse?

He leaned his head back against the seat and closed his eyes. He opened them again, rested his hands on the steering wheel and stared out the windshield. But the Bel Air just sat there, idling.

All at once, Dusty was overcome with the realization that he had a job to do. Without another thought, he twisted around in his seat and threw it into reverse.

Once in the street, Dusty slowly made his way east toward Edgewater Park. He watched the way the road followed the lake, with the houses strung along one side, as he continued toward downtown.

Traffic sped past him and someone behind him leaned on the horn.

Dusty spotted a police cruiser parked on the other side of the street as he waited at the light. He tried to be inconspicuous, hoping that he might pass for a short man driving the Bel Aire. He held his breath.

The light turned green and Dusty exhaled as he stepped on the gas again.

~ Fifty-Two ~

WINK NOTICED THAT the Bel Aire was not in the garage when he was dropped off at the house after his shift was over. He had asked for special permission to leave early. He smiled and glanced at his watch, noting that it was noon.

Wink was pleased with the fact that his plan appeared to be working. Irene was helping with the Christmas Party at the Children's Home. She would stay at the party until about 6.

Perfect.

Vast strings of bulky lights, buried deep in the branches of the tree, filled the living room with a delicious warm fragrance.

Pine boughs draped on the bannister and the sweet-scented wreath that hung over the fireplace served as a reminder that the time had come.

He looked on the kitchen table for a note from Irene. There wasn't one.

It was the day before Christmas; he and Dusty had a couple hours left in the day to get the lights strung. He had managed to get the hooks up, along the front edge of the roof, during the past few days without Irene noticing.

After an hour had passed by, Wink realized that Dusty apparently was not coming. His spirits plummeted.

Unusual for that kid; he was so responsible.

Wink reassured himself. He knew he could do it alone; after all, that had been the original plan. He would just have to improvise … *and move fast.*

He bounded down the stairs and out the door to the garage. There was some serious work to do.

Wink pulled out case after case of opened boxes of lights, strung in a kaleidoscope of colors.

Stringing the lights on the house went much faster than he had thought it would. There were existing hooks around the border of the top of the porch off the courtyard, probably put there years ago, maybe for a similar purpose.

Wink stepped back, squinted his eyes and gave it an appraisal. To him, it looked like something from the cover of *Life* magazine.

Little did Wink know that Irene was downtown, waiting at the station, for a bus to Pittsburgh.

~ Fifty-Three ~

DUSTY GRIPPED THE STEERING WHEEL so tightly, his fingers were throbbing. He swerved, just barely avoiding a blue sedan, parked on Carnegie Avenue, in front of the theatre. He accelerated and made the turn onto Euclid.

"*Road Hog!*" the man yelled at him as he passed him up, leaving him in a fresh cloud of exhaust.

Dusty slammed on the brakes. The Bel Aire fishtailed on the icy blacktop and skidded to a stop. The headlights pointed out a bright red stop sign.

He thought about turning the car around. The urge to return to the house and get Mr. Cunningham was so strong, it sent a sense of desperation through his eleven-year-old body.

Besides, he really didn't know how to drive a car. The skills he had acquired on those "illegal" Sunday afternoons along the deserted, lakefront airport road, when Wink allowed him to drive the Bel Aire, hadn't been quite enough to instill him with the confidence to tackle downtown Cleveland traffic.

Then Dusty remembered Mrs. Cunningham's letter. There was no time.

He summoned the courage to continue on his mission.

The two-tone red Bel Aire stood out like a beacon amid the ocean of plain dark sedans that populated the streets of downtown Cleveland.

Dusty stopped the car again, at the light, three blocks from the bus station. He glared at his reflection in the rearview mirror.

He glanced sideways at Mr. Cunningham's hat, resting on the passenger seat. He picked it up and placed the cover on his own head. He looked at himself in the vanity mirror and he grinned.

Dusty pulled hard on the brim of the cover to secure it on his head. He waited for a truck to pass.

Another car sped past him.

He peered over his shoulder. The light turned green and he shifted the Bel Aire into drive.

~ Fifty-Four ~

THE LAST THING SHE EVER expected she would be doing at Christmas was leaving town amidst the swirl of a raging Cleveland blizzard; this one heavier than last years'. Irene swallowed back a knot of emotion growing inside of her.

The bus station appeared behind a curtain of snow, nearly invisible in the whiteout.

Irene paid the cab driver and peered back at the Cleveland cityscape, snow flying about her face.

She recalled the early years with Wink, when he just couldn't get enough of her. Irene opened the door and found herself in front of the ticket window. She set her suitcase on the floor and opened her bag.

Irene looked at the clerk with a kind of weariness. "I need a ticket to Pittsburgh, Pennsylvania, please."

She felt the eyes behind the lenses assessing her. "Round trip?"

She shook her head, "One way only. I'm not coming back."

NOT QUITE A BLOCK AWAY, Dusty noticed a pair of headlights, dim through the blowing snow, keeping pace with him. It could have been just a cautious driver, given the weather, but Dusty's radar was on high alert.

The driver fell back and flashed his headlights at him, but Dusty sped up; he could see the bus station, just ahead.

The Bel Aire skidded into the parking lot, performing a quick one-eighty and stopped. He'd felt a tire give and he was pretty sure he'd done some damage – to the car and the parking lot.

The phantom vehicle followed the Bel Aire into the lot. Luckily, it was relatively empty and hardly noticeable that, in his haste, Dusty had parked like a drunken sailor.

In his desperate rush to get to Irene, he also hadn't noticed that another pair of headlights, farther back, had broken through the curtain of snow, coming down Chester Avenue tailing the first car. And that one was followed by yet another.

Dusty turned off the engine, grabbed the keys and ran for the building. He took a deep breath, counted to three, and entered the bus station.

HE SAW HER as he pushed the heavy door open. She was sitting on a long, wooden bench, with her brown leather suitcase beside her.

He suddenly realized that he had no idea what he was going to say to her. How in the world was he going to get Irene to go home?

She smiled up at Dusty, but her eyes were troubled.

~ Fifty-Five ~

THE ENTOURAGE BURST into the bus station parking lot amid a frenzy of red flashing lights and screaming sirens.

With desperation in his voice that was impossible to ignore, Dusty grabbed Irene's arm and shouted out,

"You have to go back home!"

Irene tilted her head to the side and was just about to say something, but he interrupted her.

"You've got to go home …now! ***PLEASE!"***

"Dusty, what are you doing here? Does your father know where you are?"

"That's exactly what I was wondering!" boomed a deep voice, brimming with disapproval. The Chief of Police approached them from behind, full support backing him up. Dusty knew he was in big trouble.

Eleven years old and in trouble with the police. But that wasn't the worst part.

Chief McBurney was his father.

Irene stood and picked up her suitcase. She looked back at Dusty and his father; in a quandary. She couldn't leave that defenseless, eleven-year-old boy to the mercy of the police department.

The chief frowned. He stepped closer and his face darkened.

But Dusty openly waved her on.

"Mr. Cunningham is in trouble ... big trouble! He needs help! Please – Go, before it's too late!!"

With Dusty's permission, Irene hastily stepped halfway into the street and waved down a taxi. The first one passed her, but the next one stopped. Irene opened the door and climbed inside.

~ Fifty-Six ~

"IT WAS AN EMERGENCY," he told his father, further skirting the lie.

Dusty knew he was skating on thin ice. You couldn't get any more regimented than Chief McBurney. His policy made no allowances for excuses. And he rarely cut anybody slack.

The police chief had taken note of the interaction between his son and the woman. He sensed a bond between them, although he had no idea what that was. Dusty's father took him by the shoulders and softened.

Chief McBurney lowered himself onto the bench next to Dusty and stared ahead, in silence. Then he turned to him.

"Would you like to explain yourself? *What in the blue blazes* is going on, son?" Dusty was usually such a good kid – the chief couldn't understand what had gotten into him.

"Chief – do you want us to take the car back to the station and call the owner?" The small army of blue waited for his response.

"No, I'll drive it back." He stood and held his hand out to Dusty for the keys. Dusty sheepishly reached into his pocket and relinquished the keys to his father, avoiding eye contact.

"But, chief – what about the report?"

He swiftly spun on his heels to face them, his neck beginning to feel warm.

"I said I would take care of it!"

This was a side of Chief McBurney nobody had ever seen before. Without a word, they fell back in line and the officer on the end opened the door for them. They watched in silence as the McBurneys exited silently to the parking lot.

"That's one kid I wouldn't want to be tonight," They shook their heads and grinned at each other as they walked back to their patrol cars.

The car door slammed shut as Dusty's father started the engine. Following its two streams of light in the dusk, the Bel Aire headed west, toward Edgeciff Drive.

~ Fifty-Seven ~

IRENE COLLAPSED INTO the seat of the taxi, anxious and eager to get back home to make sure Wink was okay.

She stared quietly out the window as she watched the city pass her by.

A couple of blocks from the bus station, she observed a young woman, kissing a young man, standing on the steps of City Hall, surrounded by dozens of people. The woman was wearing a beautiful white dress, covered by a white woolen short coat. A white, pill-box hat sat on her head. She was holding a spray of red roses, held together with a white satin bow. A man snapped a photograph.

Irene smiled. *How wonderful – a Christmas Eve Wedding!*

But then Irene's eyes widened. The groom was in full dress uniform – *blues* – Irene instantly craned around to look out the back window of the cab as the scene passed them by. The groom looked familiar.

The woman was indeed, a Christmas Eve bride. She had just been married. Then she recognized the groom.

Brian; Brian Nelson... from the fire house! I didn't even know he was engaged. Irene did a double-take as she got a closer look at the beautiful young woman.

Irene had a remarkable memory, and she never forgot a face.

She gasped.

"Oh no," she screamed and slapped her hand over her mouth as she realized what had happened. It was the same young woman who she had seen with Wink over the last month or so.

All of the pieces of the puzzle fell into place. Wink must have introduced the two. And of course they would have embraced when she told him she was engaged to be married!

Irene felt foolish. But still – why all the secrecy?

It didn't matter anymore; she had to get to Wink. She was overcome with a new sense of worry. If something had happened to him, she'd never be able to forgive herself.

~ Fifty-Eight ~

DUSK HAD SETTLED OVER the city. Streetlights began dotting the horizon.

Almost finished stringing the lights on the house, Wink ducked under the overhang as the snow continued to pile up on the roof.

He clenched his jacket closed at the neck and he tried to gauge the time from the sky.

Something cold and wet slobbered his hand. He looked down at Clancy, her tail wagging feverishly. He reached and scratched the Retriever behind the ears and he smiled.

"Well, at least *you* didn't stand me up today, girl. I guess I'll have to take you back home in a little while, won't I?"

A cab pulled up and stopped across the street from the house.

Irene climbed out and saw Wink under the eaves, wrapping the end of a light string around a hook. Now she was really confused.

He looked alright to her. What did Dusty think he was doing by lying to her?

Wink glanced across the street and saw her standing there. He walked slowly to the driveway, with a big smile.

For a moment, all she could see in the man facing her was the 18 year-old boy she had fallen in love with.

He watched silently as Irene approached him.

Wind whistled around her, bringing with it an instant chill.

"Where've you been? I was beginning to get worried."

Irene stood still, unable to move forward.

He took a half step toward her, the faintest glint of humor in his eyes. "Don't worry, I don't bite."

Irene ran to him, weeping; she flung herself into his arms.

He stood steady and wrapped his arms around her, his cheek on her hair.

She shivered in the frigid breeze off the lake.

"Just be still, would you?" he said, catching her eye with a wink as he dabbed around her puffy eyes with his bare hand. Wink leaned in and studied her face.

His scarf smelled like him. Intoxicated, she reeled as he took it off and wrapped her neck in its cocoon.

"I'm sorry," she sobbed quietly. "I've been so wrong … about everything."

He pressed his lips against the curve of her jaw. "I don't know what's been happening lately; why you've been so unhappy. Or why you came home in a taxi tonight …"

His warm breath felt good against her frozen face. Then he touched her cheek; just like the first time. The memory of that caress brought instant color to Irene's face.

"But I have never been happier to see anybody in my whole life."

She turned her head away, so he couldn't see the pain in her eyes. He nuzzled against her neck and whispered to her. "What do you say? A guy's *got* to have a date for Christmas."

"How about it?"

Irene answered him by punching his upper arm, and sobbing. Her icy fingers were trembling. He grabbed her hand and pushed it under the fold of his jacket, shoving it inside his shirt.

Until it rested on his chest. She opened her fist. Irene could feel his heartbeat.

She followed and did the same. She read a tenderness in his gaze as his eyes held hers prisoner.

The sun had dropped on the horizon, enough for the lights to begin to show against the purple indigo backdrop. It was impossible to ignore.

Irene turned toward the house. Her jaw dropped. Her eyes sparkled with tiny reflections of the lights.

"Why didn't you tell me about all this? I thought you…"

"I wanted to surprise you … and give you something you'd never forget."

She closed her eyes and nodded. "And I've been horrible."

"Don't say that," he whispered, stepping closer to her.

Irene said, "Maybe it's the writer in me that made me jump to conclusions."

Wink took Irene by the hand and led her to the side yard, to show her how he had decorated the courtyard.

She sniffled and continued. "I should have known that you had other things on your mind; that the world doesn't always have to revolve around me."

Wink interrupted her. "No, I think you made me realize all the more how much you mean to me. And that, even though I never meant to, maybe I *was* neglecting you, just a little bit."

He lowered his mouth to hers and whispered, "Just giving you fair warning …" The dimple in his cheek winked in and out.

"I'm about to take advantage of this situation."

His mouth settled gently over hers; before she could stop herself, she yielded to him.

~ Fifty-Nine ~

CHIEF MCBURNEY MADE the turn onto Edgecliff and stopped the Bel Aire in front of the house.

"Dad – Please let me talk to Wink before you come over. *Please?*"

"First of all, son, the man's name is Mr. Cunningham."

Dusty's spirits took a nosedive.

His father turned him to face him. "Look – I will park the car on the street and walk home to explain to your mother what has happened. That's my Christmas present to you. But I am coming right back for you. Believe me – you are in so much trouble with the law, if Mr. Cunningham wants to press charges."

He shook his head as he pushed the keys to the Bel Aire hard into Dusty's hand. He continued, "I don't know where you've been getting all these foolish notions."

As he started walking away; Dusty heard him mutter,

"How could such a good kid turn into a juvenile delinquent in just a couple of hours?"

~ Sixty ~

UNBEKNOWNST TO WINK and Irene, Dusty had climbed the ladder at the side of the house and scaled the treacherous roofs, through the ice and snow and was heading toward the peak.

This is all my fault!

Clancy was barking at the side of the house, then she dashed to the front, continuing to bark up at the roof, becoming more frantic the higher the boy climbed.

The star was not lit. It hadn't even been plugged into the outlet yet.

Just as he stretched to make the cord for the star reach the outlet, he lost his footing. The cord ripped away from the base of the star and he slid down the roof, tumbling to the edge, barely able to hang on at the lip.

Dusty was devastated – he thought he had failed, the whole point was to show off the beautiful star the captain and Wink had created, together.

The dog continued to bark wildly, darting to the driveway and tugging hard at Wink's jacket, pulling him with incredible strength.

Irene and Wink stared down at the usually docile pup and realized that something was wrong.

"What is it, Clancy? What's wrong, girl?" Clancy ran to the side of the house, with Wink and Irene in hot pursuit.

Then they spotted him.

Irene screamed. "Dusty!!"

Wink rushed to retrieve the fallen ladder to rescue Dusty.

He reached him on the third rooftop while Irene and the dog nervously watched from below.

"Hang on, kid! - I'm almost there!"

He could see the fear growing in Dusty's eyes as the boy dangled from the eaves like the clapper of a bell, in the wintry breeze off Lake Erie. Clancy nervously clawed at the ladder, as if she wanted to climb it. Wink calmly looked down and, in a reassuring tone, he told her,

"It's okay, Clancy. Calm down ... *calm down* ... "

She stopped, except for a little whimper. Wink smiled downward and praised her. "That's a girl ... *Good girl.*"

"Dusty – don't look down. Everything is going to be alright."

But just as he pulled Dusty back up onto the safety of the peak, his foot slid and the boy slipped from his grip.

Wink quickly leaped from the low edge of the roof and landed brutally, splits-style, onto the top rung of the ladder.

Wink grunted in pain, then quickly hooked one booted foot over the top rung of the ladder. He stretched out and gripped the sleeve of Dusty's jacket and pulled him back over the edge, preventing him from tumbling to the ice-covered patio below.

They both lay on their backs, facing up into the sky, sighing deeply with relief.

"Dusty, what on Earth were you doing?"

The boy sniffled as he spoke, his eyes closed. He felt defeated, and disappointed in himself.

"I'm so sorry. I know you needed me to help you today, but I let you down. You wanted everything to work – *and the star* ... It was supposed to light up. I wanted the star to light, too. – *I wanted it real bad*. For the captain and for you."

Dusty's father had just rounded the corner, stepping up his speed when he realized that the small shadow up on the rooftop with Mr. Cunningham was his son. He ran to the yard and joined Irene.

Wink sat up and gently pulled the boy along with him. He firmly placed his hands on Dusty's shoulders. He leaned over with an empathetic yet prudent expression on his face.

"Listen, Dusty - you've got to let go of this wild idea about *the captain*." He hesitated for a moment before continuing.

"I know sometimes it's fun to believe. But you've just got to let it go. He's gone. He just doesn't exist … *anymore*."

"No!" Dusty broke loose from his grip and crawled across the surface of the roof. He slowly inched closer until he found himself in front of the star.

Dusty was disheartened. He stood and stared out at the lake, then into the sky. Any hope he had that the star would light had been thrown against the rocky edges of the Edgewater shoreline. He dropped to his knees and he cried.

But as he turned to crawl away, the star slowly began to glow, lighting one struggling, faint bulb at a time, increasing in intensity as each caught on, until the star was completely lit up, in a full blown glittery magnificence.

Without any power being supplied to it.

Dusty gasped. *"Look!"*

Wink turned his head. He edged over, dodging icy patches on the roof and stopped. He leaned over to Dusty.

"But it's not plugged in. How can that be?"

Dusty looked up at Wink, and stood, a slow smile creeping across his face.

"Maybe it's because I ***believe****."*

It sounded far-fetched to Wink but he was running out of explanations, and that was just as logical as anything else he could think of.

Wink noticed something he hadn't seen before; a faded pattern etched into the stone chimney, freshly illuminated by the newly lit star. He traced the pattern with his fingers.

Spellbound, he whispered to himself,

"It's a Compass Rose!"

And then, by the warmth from the light of the luminary, it dawned on them. They both understood something about the beautifully lit Christmas star, hanging on the chimney.

It was a Compass Rose, too. It had been all along; it just needed the right person to finish what the captain had started, years ago.

Wink looked down and saw Irene and the chief of police, along with about a dozen people standing in the yard below, some bundled up in winter attire; one was dressed only in pajamas, slippers and earmuffs. He saw Jacques Laurent and the woman who had been fishing from the pier, months ago. They were standing together, smiling. Mrs. Petrie and the General were holding hands.

Who would have thought ...?

Wink was no longer alarmed at the surprises and things people knew on the street, or underestimated their loyalty.

He guided Dusty back to the ladder and they descended down to the courtyard. Clancy's tail wagged wildly as she waited for Dusty to pet her. His father hugged him.

"Maybe you could teach me a thing or two. I am very proud of you, son."

Irene ran through the snow drift to Wink, wrapping her arms around him. She pulled back slightly, with worry, and asked him,

"Are you alright?"

He winked at her and answered with a half-hearted chuckle, "Oh, I'm fine. Although I may never be able to father children."

Irene smiled. She whispered in his ear, "Maybe you'll just have to try harder."

Wink turned back toward the house and stopped. He took a good look around at the eclectic collection of Christmas Eve characters that had assembled in his yard. He couldn't help his thoughts.

And they all live in my neighborhood.

How lucky for me.

~ Sixty-One ~

SHE SAT ON HER HAUNCHES and stared at him. Dusty looked away.

Clancy's gaze remained, unwavering. He rubbed the Dog's head with his shoeless foot.

She was up on her hind legs, howling and making all kinds of commotion.

The dog was restless; she yipped and yapped and acted like she needed to go out. When that didn't work, she let out one big *woof.*

His mom and dad had gone to bed. Frustrated, Dusty pulled his boots on again and headed for the back door. He grabbed the dog's leash, the door flew open and the duo started down the steps to the driveway.

The sky above the lake was bursting with stars.

Dusty and his father had just gotten in the door only a half hour ago. He was thankful that his parents agreed to wait until after Christmas to decide what his punishment would be. Wink was adamant that Dusty not be punished and the chief had agreed, but he wasn't going to let Dusty know that; better that he think about it for a few days.

As soon as Dusty attached Clancy's leash to her collar, the Retriever began pulling and dragging him toward Edgecliff. When the Cunningham house was in sight, she picked up momentum.

Clancy plowed through the snow-covered rose garden at the side of the house, a mortified, breathless Dusty in tow.

"Hey, Girl – *slow down.*"

She refused to listen and had Dusty trotting at a fast clip to barely keep up with her. As they approached the top of the hill, Clancy's leash broke loose from Dusty's grip. The dog never hesitated and playfully bounded down the rocky cliff.

Raking his fingers through his hair, Dusty stopped at the steps and looked back at the Cunningham house, hoping that Wink might still be up – he would help him. Clancy *loved* Wink.

He froze. He wondered …

Dusty whirled back around. Sure enough, just as he'd thought – Clancy was tracking something. She sat, concentrating and shut the rest of the world out.

The dog lifted her nose into the air and sniffed. It was like the wind was bringing an important message. Clancy's brain was picking up smells in layers, waiting for the answer of who was nearby.

Human sweat, aftershave, cigarette smoke. That's when she knew for certain somebody was down on the beach again.

And so did Dusty.

Someone was out there; a silvery ghost of a man, facing the lake, pacing back and forth, creating a path in the fresh snow. In the pale blue moonlight, he looked almost transparent.

Smoking a cigarette, as if it gave him comfort, he stared out across the lake, in the direction of Canada.

He looked so old and gaunt. And tired; so very tired. A gaze of melancholy settled over him.

Without warning, Clancy bounced, playfully, stopping just behind the man. She picked up a stick in her mouth; then she let out a whine.

Hearing the dog's whimper, the man looked back at Clancy – he took the stick and gently threw it across the snow-covered beach. Clancy took off after the stick.

Then the man looked over at Dusty.

He was miserable, his shoulders hunched, eyes sad, and then he looked away.

The breeze chilled Dusty to the bone. He put his icy hands in his pockets for comfort. His eyes widened. He pulled out the pendant from his right pocket. His hand warmed instantly.

It was then that Dusty knew who the man on the beach was.

He was the old man who had been the caretaker of the house for years; old man Hutchinson. But that wasn't all.

He was also John Stockton. Captain John Stockton. He was sure of it.

Dusty stood on the rocky cliff, above the beach. He inched closer to the edge. He held his closed hand out to the captain and slowly opened his trembling fingers, exposing the Compass Rose.

The captain stared at Dusty as if *he* was the apparition.

"Go on, take it – *Please!"*

The man took the cigarette out of his mouth and stared at it. Then he threw it to the ground and stomped on it. He turned to face Dusty, with sadness in his eyes; then he looked away and continued on his way along the beach, toward the lake.

But Dusty, still perched on the edge of the rocks, shouted out to him; he was on the verge of tears.

"Captain!"

The man stopped again; he turned and looked back at Dusty. He cocked his head to one side.

Dusty stumbled as he hastily slipped down the steep, rocky slope to the beach, tearing the sleeve of his jacket, but he never lost a beat. He jumped back up, bravely running, full-speed, toward the stranger.

He continued, knowing that he could fall on the ice and snow, losing his footing at any moment. Dusty sprinted as if he had wings and caught up with the man.

They were face-to-face.

"Captain Stockton!" Dusty swallowed hard. His voice cracked as he held out his open hand to the man again.

"Take the Compass Rose. *It belongs to you.*"

The captain just looked past Dusty; his eyes rimmed with emptiness, as if his heart had been broken all over again.

It was like he didn't even hear him. He began to walk away.

Then Dusty said, in a voice somewhere between a whisper and a shout, "It belongs to *Kathleen.*"

The captain stopped and slowly turned to face him again. He blinked as if the gesture surprised him.

A lightness came to his face. And he opened his hand.

Dusty took a few steps toward the man and placed the necklace in his palm.

John Stockton closed his fingers around Dusty's hand.

His hand, while it had initially felt cold to Dusty, warmed considerably as the captain turned it into a firm handshake.

He supposed he should have been afraid, because that's how eleven year-old boys are, but he wasn't.

Something had pulled Dusty there; to the Edgewater shore, for a reason. And that reason had to be Captain John Stockton.

"It's all good now, isn't it?" Dusty's eyes met the twinkle in the man's eyes as he nodded back to him.

John Stockton turned to walk away, but suddenly spun back and clearly mouthed the words,

"Thank you."

~ Sixty-Two ~

THE MOON CAST a reflective glow across the lake between downtown and the beach at Edgewater.

A tiny, antiquated boat approached the shore. The outboard motor died completely as the vessel drifted closer.

The boat butted gently against the rocks. An anchor dropped into the shallow water. Lake Erie wasn't frozen, but there were chunks of ice that separated as it swayed back and forth.

A man climbed out and waded in the direction of Edgewater Beach, then he leaped onto the rocky shore, His gait was slow and measured.

He stopped, pressing his booted foot against a large rock. He held out a hand toward the man on the shore.

"Good evening, captain. We've been waiting for you."

Captain Stockton turned and faced Dusty. His eyes bored into him with a slight smile; a look of anticipation.

Then he pulled down on the bill of his hat. He spun on his heels, took the man's hand and walked onto the rocks, against the wind, in the direction of the boat.

Dusty wondered why the captain of a big ship would be picked up by a dinghy.

Then he remembered that a ship would not be able to get close to the shore … a smaller vessel always transported the passengers out to deeper waters.

Dusty was stunned as he watched the image of the boat and the two men shrink in size until it was nearly impossible to see anymore.

~ Sixty-Three ~

DUSTY SHOT OFF LIKE a rocket, toward the front of the house and flew to the door to alert Wink, ringing the bell, incessantly.

When Wink answered the door, Dusty was unable to think of what to say.

He finally blurted out, "We've got to get to the telescope. Now! Hurry!!"

Wink didn't take the time to grab a coat; he just pulled the keys to the garage from his pocket as he blindly followed Dusty, who was chattering so fast he couldn't understand much of what he was saying.

As they approached the garage, Wink asked him, "What do you mean you saw Captain Stockton? What happened?"

Dusty stopped. His memory of the incident was fading.

He wished to hell he could remember what exactly had happened between them, but he couldn't. All he knew for sure was that he actually had the encounter with him. Dusty stopped and looked at the ground.

"You don't believe me, do you?"

Wink placed his arm around Dusty's shoulder and assured him, "I believe, kid … for the first time in a long while, I *believe*." He unlocked the door to the garage and headed to the back.

They knew how cold it would be up there, but it didn't matter.

Something deep inside propelled them up the steps of the carriage house to the attic. They raced up the stairs and scrambled over to the telescope, taking turns looking thru the eyepiece.

They watched, in awe.

Far off the coast of Edgewater Beach, the captain boarded a large ship. Then, as if he knew he was being watched, he turned and faced the shore. The ship's horn sounded deeply, a distant moan, a little a foghorn.

Captain John Stockton placed his hands in his pockets.

Lights from another vessel cut through the night air, approaching the ship from the east. A man stepped onto the ship's bow and turned back to the boat, holding out his hand to assist his passenger boarding the ship.

She was breathtaking; dressed in a sapphire blue damask party dress that dusted the ship's deck. It was difficult to say if she walked or floated on air as she joined the captain. At first, it was impossible to identify her face.

Then the captain pulled something from his pocket.

The necklace; the Compass Rose pendant. She turned to face the Edgewater shore, holding up the stray wisps of her hair as he stood behind her and fastened it around her neck.

It was Kathleen, in the same dress she was wearing in the painting.

Kathleen took the captain's hand. With her touch, he transformed into the handsome sea captain who had swept her off her feet, more than forty years ago.

Then they turned away and vanished from sight.

The ship made a turn, heading for deeper waters … then it faded into the night sky.

But not before Wink made out the weathered name on the ship's side.

The Compass Rose.

SHORTLY AFTER MIDNIGHT, Wink bundled up and headed outside to turn off the Christmas lights.

Before he returned to the house, he paused to admire the beautiful lakeshore view of the city, deep in thought.

Captain Stockton had been a ship without an anchor – for a long, long time.

And, just as a ship's crew needed its captain, the captain needed his ship …

… To find his way home.

~ Sixty-Four ~

WINK TOSSED AND TURNED in his sleep.

The water surrounding the raft was filled with bullets and spurting fountains of water amid ricocheting metal shrapnel. The tiny raft tipped and swayed, taking on water at a fast rate.

He struggled against the blood-soaked bags, weighing him down, fighting off the nauseating metallic taste in his mouth.

As he emerged, he let out a strangled cough. He gasped for fresh air.

His bruised and bloodied face searched frantically for the pilot, his only survivor. Ears ringing, he shoved his arms up over them, attempting to escape from the pain. The agony in his joints was so intense that he didn't think he would ever be able to bring his arms back to his sides. He squeezed his eyes shut and tried to talk himself out of a breakdown.

After about 5 minutes, the sea calmed. He looked down at his right hand. More hope fleeted away; the compass needle had frozen.

Wink lay motionless on the floor of the raft, staring up at the gray sky, shrouded by gloomy, fast-moving clouds.

And he waited.

He was convinced that the low, thick cloud ceiling was playing a big part in keeping him hidden; alive. He checked the pilot again for a pulse. He was still breathing, but fading. He thought he spotted a B-25, but it didn't see them.

His flare gun was worthless; his compass had frozen. What else could go wrong?

Wink had just about run out of hope. He felt himself collapse against the side of the raft, leaning over the edge, his fingers digging into the side.

He listened to nondescript sea life rubbing along the raft bottom.

How long would it be before the sharks found them?

Wink's delirious mind played tricks on him for the next few moments; he heard the sea claiming him ... calling his name.

He imagined, or dreamed, being snatched back, off the one-way path leading to the Pacific floor burial ground.

"... not on our watch, Cunningham ..." The trailing voice echoed.

The sky was dark. Lightning bolts hit the atmosphere as thunder in the distance continued in deafening waves.

Winston was reeling, his head in a heavy cloud, as if he had been drugged. Water crested over the sides of the raft, sloshing over everything in its way, while eerie visions floated past him.

Vague words smeared across the side of the broken plane, then disappeared, only to reappear again, as the waves of sea mist and fog thickened, like pea soup. His brain struggled to unscramble the letters.

... The ... SS ...

... SS... something, or ... something ...SS ...

"WHAT??!"

Wink's eyes flew open. He shot up into a sitting position, cold sweat pouring down his face.

Half-asleep, Irene sat up next to him, gently rubbing his back. "You had it again, didn't you? The dream."

She smiled sleepily at him and guided him back on the bed. He pulled her tight against him and he drifted back to sleep.

~ Sixty-Five ~

IT REALLY DIDN'T SURPRISE Wink Cunningham, when the call came in shortly after dawn, on Christmas Day, 1954.

At 2:18 am, EST, The United States Coast Guard had reported the spotting of an abandoned shipwreck, off the southern coast of Florida. It appeared to be that of a merchant ship, registered in Cleveland, Ohio USA, that had been reported missing and presumed lost, with her 28 man crew, in September of 1926. It had remained a mystery, with no sign of the vessel, her crew, or any clue as to her fate.

Maritime legend had it that she had been lost forever, heartbroken, without her only love; her captain who was not onboard for her fateful, final journey.

It had been her one and only voyage he was not present for.

News of the discovery spread like wildfire throughout the nautical community and echoed back to Cleveland, Ohio.

The US Coast Guard met Wink at the 9th Street Pier, with more details of the news, just before 11:00 am.

Lieutenant Theodore Anderson extended his hand to Wink as he approached.

"Pleasure to meet you, Sir."

Wink shook his hand and replied,

"That's quite a discovery you've found. Did you say it's been missing since 1926?"

The officer nodded and added, "September 1926, to be exact."

The two walked along the pier, back toward the shore. He continued,

"Now and then, an underwater archaeologist comes up with a theory about where she might be resting, but it has never panned out to be anything."

"Until now."

Up until that point, Wink had assumed that the reason the Coast Guard contacted him about the discovery of the shipwreck was that he'd shown so much interest in local maritime history.

But Wink was surprised to learn that there was a different reason he had been contacted that early Christmas morning; another purpose they were there.

"We have reason to believe this might belong to you." The Lieutenant studied Wink's face intently as he handed over a small, brown envelope to him.

Curious, Wink hastily tore open the seal and turned the envelope upside down, emptying its contents, on a chain, into his hand.

He immediately stiffened. He held it up to the light to read the engraving on the small silver metal rectangles that hung from the chain.

"It was found hanging on the ship's wheel," Lieutenant told him.

Wink was holding his dog tags. The tags he had lost in 1945, at sea. They sent him sailing back in time. His mind drifted.

The dream … it was coming back to him again. But this time, he was wide awake.

In this vision, he finally recalled the obscure outline of two men hovering over him after pulling him from the sea, then gently returning his limp, soaking wet body back to the raft. One of the men spoke to him softly.

"Not on ***our*** watch, Cunningham. We need you."

As Wink lay lifeless, he had been much too weak to process what had happened aboard that tiny raft, fighting for his life.

But it was 1954 now, and he was recalling so much more in vivid detail. His lips pressed together and he swallowed hard.

At last - he was remembering.

Another detail flowed back to him. Wink's heart skipped a beat. He could see it playing out in his head.

The man who spoke to him aboard the raft, firmly placed something in Wink's palm, then he pulled his hand back. He was missing his index finger.

Except this all had to have happened *before* he was rescued by the Navy. Wink raked his fingers through his hair and leaned against the Coast Guard truck.

And then he remembered seeing the words on the fuselage of the broken plane as it had passed him by, on the Pacific Ocean.

Wink swallowed the lump in his throat as his mind replayed the recurring scene.

Vague words smudged across the side of the broken plane, then disappeared; only to reappear again, amid the waves of sea mist and thickening fog.

Water lapped rhythmically against the raft while the air, heavy, like pea soup, dropped over the sides with each dip.

Memories flashed back like lightning. The recollection was clearing.

As the sun momentarily pierced the hazy mist, Wink watched a steamship approach, on a direct collision course with his raft.

Too weak to fight, he braced himself for the impact.

And then the ship vanished.

It never was the plane.

Wink felt chills that ran from the tips of his fingers, clear down to his toes.

The vessel had gotten so close - *damn close.*

Close enough for him to make out a little more of the washed-out name on the ship's bow.

... SS... something, or ... something ... SS ...

Wink closed his eyes and swayed off-balance as his mind continued to slowly peel back the layers of fog.

"Sir, are you alright? You're sweating. Do you need a doctor?" Lieutenant Anderson reached out to steady him.

Eyes still shut, Wink inhaled deeply and then he exhaled. Finally, the weathered block letters revealed themselves, one-by-one; in order. He opened his eyes and turned to the Lieutenant.

"You never told me the name of the ship that was discovered this morning."

"I didn't? Oh, I'm sorry, Mr. Cunningham." The officer turned the document so Wink could read it. His eyes grew wider as he read the name of the ship at the top of the paper.

That was when Wink knew he would never have the dream again. The mystery had been solved.

The boat with the two men aboard who had pulled him out of the Pacific in 1945, and the abandoned vessel discovered that morning that had been lost in 1926, were one in the same.

The Compass Rose.

About Nancy Elvira

Nancy Elvira is a native Ohioan, born and raised on the North Coast.

The Compass and the Rose **is** the second book in ***The Edgewater*** series of novels.

Nancy has worked as an IT Coordinator, editor, award-winning photographer, confectionery artist and a librarian. Her flair for storytelling was discovered after uncovering quirky local historical facts during a research project.

When she's not writing, she replenishes harmony and tranquility in her life by spending time with her family and exploring the outdoors.